Cubana

Cubana

JaQuavis Coleman

www.urbanbooks.net

Urban Books, LLC
300 Farmingdale Road, N.Y.-Route 109
Farmingdale, NY 11735

ISBN 13: 978-1-64556-137-8
ISBN 10: 1-64556-137-2

First Trade Paperback Printing November 2020
Printed in the United States of America

10 9 8 7 6 5 4 3 2 1

Distributed by Kensington Publishing Corp.
Submit Orders to:
Customer Service
400 Hahn Road
Westminster, MD 21157-4627
Phone: 1-800-733-3000
Fax: 1-800-659-2436

Cubana

by

JaQuavis Coleman

Prologue

Duality

Five little monkeys jumping on the bed
One fell off and bumped his head
Mama called the doctor, and the doctor said
No more . . . monkeys . . . jumping on the bed

The young child gleefully sang the lullaby as she smiled, playing patty-cake with her imaginary friend. A little brown girl sat Indian style on the floor, wearing a long, white pajama gown. Her skin was ebony, but her eyes . . . Her eyes were ice-cold blue—a rare combination; however, a beautiful one. Her angelic voice echoed through the sparsely furnished house. Four pigtails hung from her head. She looked to be no older than 6 or 7 years old. She continued to sing the children's song, merrily clapping the air as if there were someone else directly in front of her. The happiness in her eyes was innocent and pure.

The open windows allowed her voice to travel onto the streets of Havana, Cuba. The dilapidated homes lined the block, which sat on a long, dirt road. Stray monkeys hopped around the streets playfully along with kids without a care in the world. The simple, familiar, lullaby was majestic and loud. It was peaceful and highlighted the Sunday morning. Loud enough for the man just outside to hear it as he walked toward the home. He had a small, leather duffle bag in his hand as he made his way toward the house. As the man approached the door, he glanced around and peeked down the block, watching while the kids played stickball in the middle of the street. He also saw young girls jump roping and others playing tag; some of them barefooted. It was a harsh but lovely sight to behold. The blissful adolescents were having so much fun, although they were impoverished, not even being able to afford the bare necessities of a simple pair of shoes. Their innocence wouldn't allow them to understand the extent of their own dire situations.

Some of the houses had openings where windows should have been. Roofs were damaged, and each house looked like it was one strong wind away from collapsing. What the city lacked in wealth, they made up for with pride and tradition. The graffiti-littered surfaces on the side of houses and buildings were ugly but also stunning—duality at its finest.

The man scanned further down the street and saw various domino matches being played at small tables. People congregated outside of some of the homes, laughing and speaking Spanish. Groups of men huddled around the small tables and hooted as the beaming hot sun seemed not to bother their golden skin complexions.

Saint Von was the man's name who scoped the neighborhood. He simply went by Saint. He was visiting from the United States . . . New Orleans, Louisiana, to be exact. Saint felt the burning sun shining down on his neck as he pulled the bucket hat down snugly onto his shiny, bald head. He tried to block the sun from his eyes and then straightened the gold-rimmed sunglasses on his face. A toothpick hung from the left side of his mouth as he twisted it using his thumb and pointer finger. He carried a small duffle bag in the other hand. Sweat beads dripped from his brow as he made his way into the house where the angel-like voice was coming from.

Saint wore an open, white linen shirt, and his tattooed body was on full display as a bulging belly somewhat stuck out over his belt buckle. Saint wasn't flabby by any means, but his belly slightly poked out and served as a trophy for his years of good living. His neatly trimmed, full beard hung down to his Adam's apple, and his bear-like face was highlighted by beautiful white teeth on the top row, with a gold row across the bottom.

Just before he stepped into the doorless home, he heard the sounds of monkeys panting and making noises just above him. It made him look up and notice the wild animals hopping around on the roof of the five-story building next door. They were moving frantically, playfully beating on their chest. He shook his head and entered the home. He couldn't get used to the wild animals blending in with society as if normal. It was a far cry from his upbringing in Nola.

As he stepped inside the house, he saw a dimly lit hall. A creaky flight of stairs was right in front of him that led to the second story of the flat. The long, dim, and damp hall was one that Saint had been in quite a few times. He had made it a habit to come to see the woman they called Pandora every time that he visited Cuba. It was always his last stop before heading back home. As he climbed the stairs, the sound of the child's voice grew louder and louder. The smell of burning incense filled Saint's nostrils as he approached the door at the top of the staircase.

As Saint entered the room, he saw the young girl on the floor, playing. He paused and then smiled as he walked past her. They locked eyes, and Saint's bright smile triggered her to return one as well. He headed toward the back where long, flowing beads separated the rooms as they hung from the door's overpass.

Saint slowly walked into the room. The sound of the beads tapping one another always soothed him. He entered. The deeper he got in the room, the less and less he heard the young girl's voice. He squinted his eyes and tried to focus on the dark figure that was in the corner. As he got closer, he heard the sound of a match being lit, and a large flash of light followed it. The flame was connected to a long, wooden matchstick, which was held by unusually long, manicured nails. Each nail was at least four inches long.

A woman's face appeared as the match's flame slightly illuminated the room. Saint's eyes locked in with hers. Her beautiful, big, penny-shaped pupils and full lips let him know exactly who it was. The familiar face soothed him as he walked closer to the light, exposing her face more clearly. The gorgeous woman before him was none other than Pandora. She wore a multicolored silk wrap around her gray locs, which hung out from the top of it.

"I've been expecting you, Saint," Pandora whispered as a small grin formed on her face. She spoke clear English but with a heavy Spanish accent. Her skin was the deepest ebony Saint had ever seen. Her eyes were a rare blue color. They were oddly gorgeous. In this beautiful country, it was a usual combination; however, the States had stripped Saint's interpretation of what Black looked and sounded like. A Black woman's physical characteristics had limitless shades and mixtures, and Pandora was the evidence of that. He was standing there in pure amazement.

Pandora was simply majestic to the naked eye. She was nearly twenty years his senior. However, one couldn't tell by her looks and smooth skin. It was when she opened her mouth that her age showed. Pure wisdom flowed from her mouth, and the strain in her voice showed her years on this earth. She proceeded to light the candles that were spread around the table where she was sitting as Saint stood before her.

"Have a seat," she instructed as she blew out the match and focused her undivided attention on him.

Saint's eyes followed the smoke from the match, and it led directly into her blue eyes. Her gaze was piercing and unwavering as she stared at him, almost as if she were looking *through* him rather than *at* him. An intense chill crept up his spine, and he felt his shoulders becoming more relaxed at the end of it. A small flutter happened in Saint's heart, and like always, he was mesmerized by her presence. He slowly took a seat and gently set the duffle bag on the hardwood floor next to his chair. Saint placed his hands on his lap and took a deep breath as the smell of burning sage and incense calmed him.

"Hey, Pandora," Saint said, as he got comfortable in his chair and looked around the room.

"Hello, handsome," she said as she strategically spread the small crystals around the table. Saint looked at the little gems as she aligned them and incoherently mumbled things under her breath. Pandora closed her eyes and slowly swayed back and forth, and then she stopped abruptly and froze. A small smile formed on her face, and she opened her eyelids, focusing directly on Saint.

"Our ancestors are ready to speak. But before we do what you came here for, let's talk. I feel something is on your heart. Something other than what's in that bag down there," she said as she nodded her head in the direction of the duffle bag full of plastic-wrapped kilos.

Saint was taken aback because it seemed as if she were reading his mind. He usually would come to get his "bricks baptized" by Pandora. He would ask her to separate any Karma or harm that would come to him by way of the bricks of heroin he was about to distribute back in the United States. However, on this particular trip, he had a few extra things going on in his life that he needed help with.

"Damn, you always seem to know what's on my mind," Saint said, shaking his head in amazement.

"No, I always know what's on your heart. I can see it through your eyes. So . . . Come on, talk to mama," Pandora said as she winked and attempted to lighten the mood. Although Pandora was highly spiritual, she had a way of making people feel comfortable with her. Her motherly spirit was one of comfort. She had a special skill for making people open to her.

"There are a few things. I ran into some legal trouble a few years back, and the case came back up. My trial starts in a few," Saint admitted.

"Oh, I see. You're on trial for what cause?"

"Murder," he answered in a low tone as his eyes dropped, breaking their gaze.

"Did you do it?" Pandora asked blatantly and without hesitation. Saint nodded his head in admittance.

"Yeah, but in self-defense," he whispered, genuinely having regret for what he had done. He had sorrow but not for defending himself. Rather, for taking the life of someone that he knew personally.

"I can see that your words are pure, and you have remorse," Pandora said, as she clasped her hands together. She paused and just stared at Saint before speaking again. You could tell that she was analyzing him and choosing her words wisely before she spoke.

"I will ask for guidance from our ancestors, and if I can help you . . . I will. You will have to come back after the sun sets," Pandora explained carefully. Saint nodded in agreement and reached down to go into his bag and placed his hand on a brick. He was about to put them on the table so Pandora could bless them, but Pandora waved her hand, signaling for him to pause.

"There is something else on your heart. What else is troubling you?" she asked as she rested her hands on top of his. Saint closed his eyes and paused, realizing that he couldn't get anything past her. He took a deep breath and sat upright. He chuckled to himself and shook his head, realizing that Pandora was very good at what she did. He couldn't get anything past her. He slightly showed the golds in his mouth with his partial smile.

"I'm getting married. Well, if I'm not in prison . . . I'll be getting married."

"Ooh, here is the *good* stuff," Pandora said playfully as she sat upright as well. "Do tell . . ." she said.

"There's really nothing to tell. Shorty is the truth. I just don't know if I'll be the man she wants me to be. I never did anything like this before," he honestly admitted.

"Okay, I see. You have cold feet, eh?" Pandora said as she nodded slowly, understanding exactly what was going on. "Well, you need some advice, not divine intervention." Pandora slowly waved her arm across the table, clearing all the stones and gems so it would be a clear pallet. She placed her hands on the table with her palms facing up.

"Come on," she instructed as she glanced down at her hands, wiggled her fingers, and then looked up at Saint. Saint placed his hands inside of hers and listened carefully, knowing that she was about to lay some game on him as she always did.

"What's your worries, Saint? Do you not love her?" Pandora asked.

"Of course, I love her. She's a real one," he admitted.

"So, if she's the one . . . Why the hesitation?"

"That's the million-dollar question. I don't know exactly. I dream about her in colors that don't exist." He paused as he let his words marinate. "She's been there with me from the beginning. I just want to reward her with everything. She deserves to be happy. She has been through it all. She held me down every single time and never once made me think she wasn't in my corner. Even when it was hard," Saint said, feeling the urge to tell Pandora every single emotion he was feeling toward his fiancée.

"Okay, so why don't you want to marry her?" she asked.

"I do. I just don't want to hurt her. My life is real, ya hear me?" Saint said as his New Orleans drawl emerged in his dialect. He was good about hiding his strong New Orleans accent, but when he spoke from the heart, it always seemed to peek its head. He continued, "This life is not fit for marriage. I'm knee-deep in this shit. I want to wait until things slow down for me so that I can focus on her. But on the flip side, I can't make her wait forever. Does this make sense?" Saint said, seeking guidance. Pandora gently squeezed his hands and took a deep breath.

"You ever lie to her, you ever lied to this woman you speak of?" Pandora asked.

"Yeah, I have. Only to protect her feelings, though," he replied.

"She's found out about these lies that we speak of?" Pandora quizzed. Saint simply nodded his head, confirming her suspicions.

"Let me tell you something about a woman, and I need you to listen closely," Pandora spoke. She paused and turned her head to the side, staring at nothing in particular, searching for the correct words.

"Be careful about lying to your woman. Every time she forgives you, you will love her a little more. However, with your lies, she will begin to love you a little less. So, the day you love her the most will be the day that she will love you the least." Those words sent shivers throughout Saint's body, and the heaviness of his heart resonated deeply within his chest.

"Now, that advice is on the house. Something to grow on," Pandora stated as she released her grasp and focused back on the crystals that were on the table. She realigned her crystals, placing them correctly. Saint thought about her words, and just that quick, he made a decision. He decided if he beat his current case, he wouldn't waste any time in marrying his woman.

Saint smiled and placed the bricks on the table as Pandora began the baptism. As always, Saint just sat back and watched. The process never took too long, and some would say it was a waste of time, but ever since his connect suggested this, he had never been pinched by the law. Therefore, he never took his chances and skipped the process. He had a routine, and it had been that way for years. He would see his connect, and, on his way out, he would always stop by and see Pandora. Some would call it superstitious, but Saint called it playing the game the way it was supposed to be played. He listened as she chanted . . .

Afterward, Saint carefully placed the bricks back into his leather bag but not before sliding an envelope filled with cash over the table to Pandora. She smiled and received the money. Saint gathered himself and his bags, then stood up. He bent down and kissed Pandora on the cheek as he always did and then headed out.

As Saint reached the door, he turned back and found Pandora looking at him while smiling. He returned the smile and proceeded out. As he glanced at the wall just by the exit, he saw writing on the wall. The word "*Duality*" was written in what seemed to be a kid's handwriting. It stood out because it wasn't a common word that a child or someone of an adolescent age would write, and the word stuck with him. Saint never used the word before, so he was somewhat unfamiliar with the term.

"The more you live . . . the more you'll understand. I'll see you after dark for that other matter," Pandora said as if she were reading his mind as he tried to ponder about the meaning.

Saint said nothing and walked out. As he entered the hallway, the sound of the young girl's voice picked back up, getting louder with each step. She was singing the same lullaby as if she had never stopped singing. Saint noticed that the sound was slightly different than what he remembered. It now sounded like multiple voices were singing the song in unison. As he entered the main room, he saw the little girl sitting on the floor. However, this time, she seemed to be sitting across from another young child. They both had the same look, same gown, and same skin tones. The other child was a boy with a short haircut.

Twins? he thought as he walked past and eyed the two. With the girl, he could see her face fully, but the other child's back was turned to him as they playfully slapped hands while singing. Saint thought it was odd. He started to second-guess his memory, knowing that there was only one girl before. He shook his head and chalked it up as a mental lapse. As he walked toward the exit, he turned back to look at the children. All of a sudden, they stopped singing, and it grew eerily silent. The little girl that faced him smiled, showing her big blue eyes. Saint smiled back, and as the young boy slowly turned around, Saint held his smile, ready to greet him as well—but when he saw him, a wave of fear and confusion swept through his body.

What the fuck? Saint thought as the smile quickly faded from his face. The young boy had no facial features—nothing. No eyes, no mouth, nose, or eyebrows. Saint's mind spun rapidly, trying to make sense of what he was seeing. He looked at the girl, and she was smiling, like there was nothing unusual about her counterpart's deformity. The faceless little boy vaguely turned his head sideways, tilting his head to the side. This freaked Saint out as he shook his head in disbelief. He hurried out and wondered what the fuck he had just seen. Just as he reached the outside and felt the rays of the sun, he leaned against the house to catch his breath. Then, once more, he heard the kids sing. Saint looked down the block and noticed that it was now empty, a far cry from the happy, energetic scene from earlier. He took a deep breath, inhaling through his nose, and briefly closing his eyes to recenter himself.

Five little monkeys jumping on the bed
One fell off and bumped his head
Mama called the doctor, and the doctor said
No more . . . monkeys . . . jumping on the bed

Saint gripped his bag tightly and headed away from the house, but the sound of something crashing against the ground startled him, making him jump back. A monkey lay there as a maroon-colored puddle of blood seeped out of its body. Horrific-looking brain matter from the monkey's skull was splattered against the ground and instantly made Saint's stomach churn. He quickly looked away, not wanting to see the gruesome sight. It seemed as if the monkey had fallen from the building to its death. Saint looked up to see a lone monkey on the top of the roof dancing around while looking down at its dead companion.

Saint hurried away as he heard his phone ringing from his bag. He retrieved the phone and looked at the caller ID. It was his right-hand man, Zoo. His phone wasn't a usual one or even an up-to-date one, for that matter. His oversized Nokia phone had a long, rubber antenna sticking from it. It was at least fifteen years old and was totally outdated. Saint used this type of phone for many reasons, but the obvious one was its lack of technology. Older phones lacked the capabilities of being traced and were much more difficult to tap remotely. The long antenna allowed him to reach anywhere completely under the radar in North or South America. No phone towers were needed to correspond with the opposite party. It was basically a ramped-up walkie-talkie, and that's the device of choice he talked business on.

"Peace," Saint said, answering.

"Peace. We good?" Zoo asked.

"Absolutely. On my way back home now."

"God is good," Zoo said, smiling through the phone.

"Amen," Saint said, as he made his way down the block, where an antique car was waiting for him.

Saint pressed the *end* button and made his way to the end of the block. He saw the male driver just down the road. He was Cuban and stood no taller than five feet. The driver was waiting for Saint patiently as he leaned against the rear of the car with his arms folded. The man had olive-colored skin and wore a straw fedora hat. He seemed to be in his early 60s. Saint used him for transportation every time he visited the country, and he escorted him around in his 1960 Ford. The driver's name was Pedro.

The car was a faded red color, and you could tell that it had been sunburned over the years. The car didn't look like much on the outside. It had various rust spots, holes, and bald tires. It had been through many harsh days, and its war wounds proved it. Nevertheless, it ran like a horse, and that's all Saint could really ask for.

As Saint got closer, the man said something in Spanish and opened the rear door, giving Saint a clear path to slide in. Saint slid in and threw his head back in the car seat, thinking about the peculiar day that he had. Something was different about today, and it gave him an eerie feeling deep within his soul.

As they cruised the Cuban roads doing fifteen miles per hour, it gave Saint time to reflect. He watched as kids chased the car and knocked on the windows. He would pass out money usually, but today was different. He kept seeing the boy's blank, deformed face. He wanted to blame it on stress, but he knew better. Something was happening. He just couldn't put his finger on it. He prided himself on having a sharp mind, but this was an occurrence that he could not wrap his thoughts around. His brain was playing tricks on him in the worst way.

Or was it?

He thought about the words of Pandora and the day's events. He looked to his left and saw the bag that would be distributed throughout the bayou, making him a quick seven figures when it was done. He wanted out, and the main reason for that was so that he could become the man that the love of his life deserved. With what he saw this day, he knew someone or "something" was trying to tell him something. He just didn't know what exactly.

A beautiful cathedral church was the setting for the day's special event. Luxury cars lined the parking lot of the historic church. It was a gathering of bosses, family, and well-respected figures throughout the bayou. Stunning, hand-crafted statues of angels peppered the marbled floors, and tall podiums were the pillars of the immaculate haven. Three months had passed, and Saint was at a major crossroads in his life. He stared at himself in the full-length mirror and straightened up his bow tie, examining it very carefully. His shiny, bald head and huge, shaped beard were flawless. His well-tailored Tom Ford suit was all white, and the Italian cut fit him impeccably. His belly had even shrunk a size or two. He hung the expensive suit very well. He looked like he stepped straight out of a *GQ* magazine.

Today was the big day. He was marrying the woman who held the key to his heart, Ramina. The room had five other men inside, all of them talking amongst each other, sipping Cognac, and prepping for their leader's new union. They all were suited as well and accented with traditional black accessories. Saint was in the presence of his groomsmen, his team. Although none of them shared the same bloodline, they were family by way of the drug game.

Saint was a boss. He was the natural leader and the sole connect to the Cuban heroin plug. Although Saint was younger than some of his men, he held the most wisdom. He moved as if he were twenty years older than his actual age. He never did anything fast. His speech, his movements, his business moves were always slow and well calculated. Saint never spoke loudly. No one ever heard him raise his voice. He did everything on his own terms and in his own tone. He controlled "the board" at all times. Saint was the man that made the operation go. He was at the top of the totem pole, and it was the best-kept secret in the bayou.

Zoo approached Saint and straightened up his tie. He then threw his arm around Saint's shoulder and leaned in to talk to him. Zoo hugged him tightly.

"Today is the day, bruh. You finally about to do it," Zoo said proudly.

Saint nodded in agreement without saying a word. He looked at Zoo through the mirror and faintly smirked at his best friend. Zoo stood about six foot and had a slim build. His skin complexion was as dark as night—so dark that he almost looked purple. He wore a neatly cut Caesar hairstyle and 360 waves wrapped around his head flawlessly. He wore Cartier frames with wood grain around the rim of the glasses. He was from Flint, Michigan, and it was very prevalent in his style. He migrated to Nola ten years before, when he went to school at Louisiana Tech on an athletic scholarship. He ended up staying after his college stint and began his new career in the drug trade. In his newfound game is where he met Saint, and they had been tight ever since. He served as the underboss to Saint and was the buffer between Saint and the rest of the wolves that the job came with. Saint was more behind-the-scenes, and he moved ghostlike.

An old saying was "if you know, you know," and this term explained Saint's entire being to the fullest. He was a quiet storm in the drug game, and not everyone knew who he was, but all the *right* people knew who he was. Saint was what you called a "street king," and, on that day, the king would finally be getting his queen.

"Mina is getting a good nigga," Zoo said, having a heart-to-heart with his partner in crime. Saint slyly slid his hands in his slacks and walked over to the window that was facing the beautiful acreage behind the church. Without even looking around the room, Saint spoke.

"Give Zoo and me a minute alone," he said in his low, deep baritone. He didn't speak loudly, but when he spoke . . . people listened. Therefore, the room cleared out immediately, and Saint waited patiently as the men exited the room. Saint casually glanced back and made sure everyone was gone and only he and Zoo occupied the room before he spoke.

After the last groomsman left and the door was closed, Saint spoke. "Zoo, I'm done," he said with conviction and without a doubt. Zoo grew a look of concern on his face and walked over to Saint, joining him by the window.

"What?" Zoo asked, not believing what he was hearing.

"I'm out. I'm flying straight. I'm done with the game," Saint said.

"Wait . . . We are just getting started. How can you pull the plug? Listen, I know you on your married man shit, but we still out here in the trenches. We ain't ready to hang it up just yet. We got the entire bayou sewn up. We can't just shut down shop like that," Zoo pleaded as he was now standing in front of Saint.

"Don't worry. I'm giving you the plug. I'm done with it. It's yours now," Saint answered.

"Don't play, bro . . ." Zoo said as a wave of excitement overcame him. He shot a look of optimism in the direction of Saint and tried to read him. Throughout the years, Saint had never introduced Zoo to his Cuban plug. He always kept them separate and went alone. However, he was at a place in his life where he had enough money to retire comfortably, and he did not need the game. He was 34 years old and was ready to build a legit life with his new wife.

"Nah, I'm serious. After I get back from the honeymoon, I'm going to introduce you to the Cuban connect. It's yours now. The whole operation is yours now. I'm out," Saint said, reconfirming his exit.

Zoo couldn't hold in his emotions. He hugged Saint so tightly and firmly, understanding that Saint had just changed his life forever. With a plug like that, the sky was the limit, and it was something that any dope boy dreamed of. Zoo nearly had tears in his eyes as he released his embrace and looked at his best friend. Unlike Saint, Zoo had no escape plan for the game. He loved everything about it. All he wanted to be was a kingpin, and he was willing to take anything that came with it. In his mind, the reward of being the number one guy outweighed the pitfalls that accompanied the position. He was eating good under Saint, but he didn't have the power or the respect of Saint. And *that's* what he yearned for.

"I won't let you down, bruh. That's my word," Zoo said with belief.

As always, Saint acted as if someone were listening, so he spoke low as he leaned forward and put his lips near Zoo's right earlobe.

"We'll fly out to Cuba, and I'll personally introduce you to Alejandro," he whispered, referring to the connect. He gently tapped Zoo's cheek and continued. "Take this mu'fucka over," He then reached over and grabbed the champagne bottle that was sitting in the bucket of ice. Zoo grabbed a champagne flute, and the sound of the cork being popped echoed throughout the room. They both shared a toast as the sound of the bell rang throughout the church, which was his signal. It was time for the ceremony to start.

"Yo, quick thing. I was going to wait, but I want to get on top of this while you're away on your honeymoon. We ran into a little problem," Zoo said as he reached into the inside pocket of his blazer. He pulled out a small Baggie. Saint's eyes went directly to it, and he noticed the stamp on the front. It had a US seal on it with words underneath it. It simply read "*Cubana*." It caught Saint's attention because that was his signature stamp that he put on his heroin. However, he could tell that it wasn't his because the logo was slightly off. He knew from the jump that it was a copycat.

"You know how the game go, beloved. Niggas gon' imitate. Don't trip on that," Saint said calmly as he grabbed the pack and studied it.

"True, but this shit killing niggas. Four people overdosed this month off this pack. The mix ain't right, man. Somebody putting some shit in the game."

"You take it to Jeremy?" Saint asked, referring to their lab technician that they had on payroll.

"Yeah, he said it's bogus. It's laced with acetyl fentanyl," Zoo responded while shaking his head.

"What's that?" Saint asked as he slightly frowned.

"Fake dope. Synthetic," said Zoo.

"Who putting this out with our stamp on it?" Saint questioned as his brows frowned.

"That's the million-dollar question, my guy. We don't know. But this shit is flooded all through the bayou."

"And you say how many people overdosed off this bullshit?" Saint said as he shook the bag in front of Zoo's face.

"Four as of last night. Plus, you know the heat that bodies bring. We don't need that type of attention," Zoo answered.

Saint instantly became concerned, and his mind put a plan together. He held the Baggie up to the light with one hand and flicked it with his index finger.

"You have to get to the bottom of this. I told you what time I'm on. I'm dead serious, beloved. This isn't my concern anymore."

"I know, I know. But you know how I get down. I'm about to start shaking shit up until I get some answers," Zoo stated. Saint knew exactly what Zoo was referring to when he said, "shaking shit up," and Saint didn't want to take the leash off Zoo. Zoo was a hothead, and Saint didn't want to exchange the hands of power while in the middle of bloodshed. He knew he would have to get to the bottom of it before he completely walked away. He wanted his exit to be smooth and quiet—not like this.

Just as Saint was about to respond, the door swung open, and a petite woman that looked to be in her late fifties came in. She had a small gray Afro, and her face was made up. She wore an evening gown that matched the accent color of the wedding. Saint swiftly placed the pack of dope inside his pocket to hide it. It was his mother.

"Hey, Ma," Saint said, hoping she didn't see what he was just holding up. He especially didn't want her to see it because of her past addiction. She had been clean for only about ten years.

"Hey, baby," she said while smiling from ear to ear. Her bright smile was on full display as she waved her son over. "Come on, now. The pastor is ready for you. It's almost time to start."

"Yes, ma'am," Saint said respectfully as he nodded his head. He watched as his mom waited for him and waved him over hastily.

"We'll talk about this later, beloved," Saint whispered to Zoo. Zoo nodded in agreement, and they both headed toward the exit and prepared to go to the main chapel.

A small-framed woman stood before the cathedral's steps as she looked up at the historic place of worship. Her green eyes and caramel skin tone made her unique, and her tattooed body only added to that. She had a small tattooed heart under her left eye that was the lone marking on her flawless face. Various tattoos covered her neck, body, and even her fingers. Over thirty-five tattoos covered her entire body, which only added flair to her distinctiveness. She had a ruggedness about herself, yet was still feminine. Her Cuban descent shined through her features, so there was no hiding her heritage. Her smoky-brown skin resembled that of the people of her native land.

Tay tried her best to tame her frazzled hair as she repeatedly rubbed it down. What once was a silky-smooth mane was now brittle, wild, and all over her head. Her tattooed hands were ashy and in need of moisturizing. A wave of embarrassment overcame her as she looked up at the beautiful church before her and then down at her attire. She wore a soiled, tight-fitting jogging suit with a small jean jacket over it. She hadn't changed clothes for a week straight. She knew that she hadn't bathed in a while and probably smelled just like she felt. Nevertheless, something seemed to pull her to that place, on that day. She had to see Saint one last time before he started his new life.

Tay had heard through the grapevine that this wedding was more than just a nuptial, but it served as his retirement party to the game. The streets were speaking, and it was a day that the bayou shut down to honor its Most Valuable Player. She heard the sound of the bells ringing and instantly felt sick to her stomach. She abruptly bent over and threw up on the church steps, dry heaving as she gripped her abdomen. She was nervous and heartbroken at the same time. She was there to see the man she was in love with marry someone else. She wanted to be happy for him, but her somewhat selfish heart wouldn't allow that to happen.

Thoughts invaded her mind, asking God why he wasn't marrying her. After all that she had been through in life, it seemed like she deserved him more. The pain of meeting her soul mate, knowing that he could never be hers, was a pain that she could never have fathomed. Most people think physical pain is the worst thing in life, but try living with regret. That is true pain because there was no real end to that feeling. Regret is everlasting. It will eat you alive quicker than any cancer known to man. She knew that she had kept things away from Saint that would make him look at her differently. Therefore, she realized that she did not deserve him. The agony of knowing that was a pain that she knew would never fade away. *Too many secrets,* she thought to herself.

She gathered herself, stood straight up as she wiped her mouth, and then took a deep breath. Slowly, she walked up the stairs and then through the humongous French-style opening. She pulled the heavy doors, parting them, and walked in. The scene was breathtaking. It was something that she would only read about in fairy tales, and she was blown away. She could hear the distinct sound of the cello playing and the chatter from the guests that occupied the chapel. As she made her way toward it, she heard the sound of footsteps echoing throughout the lobby. She turned back and saw a man walking her way. He was barely paying attention to her as he made his way toward the chapel as well. As the man got closer, she saw and instantly noticed that it was one of Saint's henchmen, Gunner. She tried to bow her head to avoid eye contact, but the man had already made out who she was.

"Tay?" Gunner said as he squinted his eyes, trying to see if it was her. The young man used to have a crush on Tay, so seeing her like that instantly saddened him.

"Hey," she said shamefully as she tried to fix her hair. She slid the hair that was over her face behind her ear and folded her arms in front of her chest.

"Damn, I haven't seen you around in a while," he said nervously as he couldn't bring himself to make eye contact with the girl that he had lusted over once before.

"I know, right?" Tay said with a forced, nervous smile. Her eyes were wavering and unsteady. She, as well, couldn't bring herself to look at the young man in the eyes. She was in the middle of a drug binge and knew that it was showing through her appearance.

He couldn't believe how bad she looked. He felt a sense of pity for her. He was embarrassed for her. He could smell the absence of cleanliness bouncing off of her and dropped his head in disbelief.

The young man looked over his shoulders to see if anyone was looking at them. Then he shook his head and focused back on Tay. "Look, you shouldn't have come here. You know that," he admitted, not wanting her to mess up his boss's big day. Everyone in the hood knew what had happened the time she was around, and she was the last person that he thought would be at the wedding.

"I know, I know. I just wanted to say congratulations. I shouldn't have come," Tay admitted, and as she brushed past him and stormed toward the exit, Gunner grabbed her by the arm, stopping her.

"Hey . . . hey. Look, take this," he said under his breath as he took his free hand and reached down into his pants pocket. He pulled out a wad of money and quickly slid a hundred-dollar bill off his rubber-banded roll. He held it up in front of Tay, between his pointer and index fingers.

Tay's eyes shot to the money, and her mind instantly started to race. She thought about the drugs she could buy with that and shoot directly into her veins for the high that she had been chasing after that entire morning. Her heart pounded, and an insatiable urge overtook her. Her hand involuntarily went to the back of her neck to tame the sudden itch that overcame her. She immediately became fidgety. She looked like a full-blown fiend, and the young hustler instantly felt terrible for her. She was his age, and to see her tweak like that was heartbreaking. It was like he could see her thought processes. It was evident that she was trying to fight the urge to take the money as she stared at it intensely. She was twitching and scratching at the same time, which was making it uncomfortable for him to watch. She was at her rock bottom, and it was apparent.

"Just take it," he whispered in a pleading voice, knowing that she needed a fix so she wouldn't get any sicker than she already was. He was a dealer of heroin, so he knew the internal battle she was going through. That same feeling that was killing her was the same one that kept him in business and paid. His only worry was that word would get back to Saint that he gave Tay money so that she could get high. However, he felt sorry for her. He just wanted to help.

Just as he was about to say something else, the doors opened, and the sunlight shined into the lobby. It was the bride coming with a group of other women through the front doors, and she was headed in their direction. It was time for the wedding.

Tay focused on the woman in the big, flowing dress. The dress was glamorous and elegant. The sheer, tube-like dress was tight fitting but opened beautifully the closer it got to the ground. She looked like an ebony mermaid. Her train dragged at least eight feet behind her, and a stylist followed her and held up the rear of the gown. Tay's heart dropped when she saw how beautiful she was. She wished deep down in her heart that she was in that beautiful dress rather than Ramina. Tears welled up in her eyes, and her bottom lip quivered. Pain filled her chest, and she felt anxious. Her breath became short, and a flutter in her heart made her feel like she was about to die right there on the marble floor. She had never felt that feeling before. She placed her hand on her chest, and it seemed like the only thing she could hear was the sound of her own breathing. It was as if the world had slowed down, and Ramina was walking in slow motion toward them. She stared at Ramina's beautiful made-up face and deep maroon lipstick and was in awe. She was absolutely beautiful.

"Come on," the young man said as he wrapped his arm around Tay. He then guided her toward the sanctuary, not wanting her to ruin the wedding. Ramina was so busy gathering herself and talking amongst her squad that she didn't even notice Tay by the chapel door. Tay and Gunner took a seat in the last row, slipping in unnoticed.

Tay glanced at the head of the church. Her eyes frantically searched for Saint, trying to locate the only man she truly ever loved. She was eager to see him. It had been almost a year since she had been in his presence, and her anxiety skyrocketed. The way that man made her feel was second to none, and no drug could compare to the high that Saint was capable of giving her. She was captivated by him and his aura. Saint was a vibe. A vibe that she couldn't get anywhere else on planet Earth. He was always calm . . . always slow motion. His voice was like violins in her mind because it never got loud or off-key. His voice soothed her. Her heart raced, just thinking about his baritone. Saint was that nigga, second to none. The most impressive trait he had was the fact that he didn't even know it. And if he did, he didn't show it. His humble demeanor made him even more appealing. She smiled, seeing him in the crisp suit. She caught a glimpse of his pearly white teeth as he and Zoo talked with each other.

"He's so handsome," she whispered as a tear involuntarily slipped down her face. She quickly wiped it away and sniffled. Although she was sad, she was happy for him because he seemed to be joyful. The look on his face told his story. He seemed as if he were content, and that was true. He had finally found peace in his life. Saint was about to exit at the top of the game, and that day served as a retirement party as well as a wedding. Tay saw the line of groomsmen and bridesmaids at the helm of the place and watched closely as Zoo and Saint smiled and whispered to each other while standing there waiting for the bride to enter. The loud sounds of the organ played, and everyone immediately stood. Everyone except Tay, that is. She sat there with her hands on her lap as the sea of guests stood up around her.

Everyone's eyes shot to the entrance and waited patiently for the woman of the hour. The sounds of the wedding song were like a dagger to her heart as she closed her eyes. Every note tugged at Tay's heart, and she thought that she would have a heart attack right then and there during the ceremony in front of everyone.

Suddenly, the large church doors swung open, revealing the bride to be. By now, the tears flowed nonstop as she started to hear the gasps and chatter. Tay chanted something incoherently under her breath as the woman made her way down the aisle. She mumbled nothings in a low tone as the tears continued to flow. She watched Ramina walk past her with her beautiful white dress. A glamorous, sheer veil was over her face, but it didn't hide it well. Her watering eyes and pretty smile were on full display as she slowly made her way to her soon-to-be husband.

Tay watched as the man that she loved waited for the woman at the end of the aisle . . . that was not her. She couldn't take the pressure and quickly slipped out the back door once the bride made it to the front of the church.

Chapter One

A Toast to the Assholes

The sound of yet another plate being dropped by the waiters erupted. The shattering sound had become a part of the party, it seemed like. That was the third plate broken during the reception. People paused for a second to look over at the mishap but continued to finish up their meals as they ate the 5-star New Orleans cuisine, compliments of the chef hired by Saint and Ramina.

"You peep what's going on, bruh?" Zoo whispered as he leaned over toward Saint as they sat at the head table. Saint listened closely and then scanned the almost full reception hall. He vaguely grinned and calmly nodded his head in agreement. Saint always chose gestures over words if he could, picking and choosing when he spoke.

"That's exactly what I thought too. I knew I wasn't tripping," Zoo said as he sat back upright and fixed his blazer and adjusted his Cartier frames. He took a sip of champagne directly from the bottle and scanned the room. Champagne was flowing, and the reception was in full swing. It had been a few hours since the wedding, and now it was time for the celebration.

The vibe was a positive one, and the sounds of smooth R&B played in the background, acting as a soundtrack for the night. The reception was only for a selected few, and it was the ending of a great night. Only Saint's closest friends, business associates, and the waitstaff were in attendance. No extras. Although the crowd was small, there was a lot of power present in the building. Saint had earned a lot of respect throughout the years. Therefore, his guest list was one of importance. A few of the soldiers from Saint's blocks were there, but the guest list was mostly criminals. It was a den of hustlers and urban legends. At least a dozen street millionaires attended, all of whom Saint supplied, making that possible.

His wedding was a meeting of the elites. Everyone who was somebody came out to pay respect to Saint. Saint got just as many farewells as he did congratulations. He was moving away from the bayou and heading away for good, and everyone that ate with him knew this. Saint was the plug and the source of many men's life aspirations. He and Ramina would ride off into the sunset, leaving the life that had afforded him his luxurious lifestyle. Saint had sucked the streets dry and saved up enough money to retire comfortably from the life. He set out a plan, and he was at its pinnacle. His exit plan was well calculated. After his honeymoon, he and Ramina would retire in Miami.

A long table stood at the head of the room, and the groomsmen and bridesmaids all accompanied the newlyweds. Food had been served, and it was time for the best man to give a speech, honoring his right-hand man. Zoo stood up and grabbed a butter knife and tapped it against the wineglass, causing a chime to sound throughout the place. Everyone stopped moving and talking. Heads turned, and all their focus was now on Zoo. The DJ lowered the music that was playing throughout the speakers, and just like that, the entire place was quiet. The only people that were moving were the waiters who were picking up the dirty dishes from the different tables throughout the room. Zoo spoke loudly so everyone could hear him.

"My name is Zoey. My friends call me Zoo, if y'all didn't already know."

"Zoooo!" someone yelled from the crowd causing Zoo to pause briefly and then look in their direction. He smiled.

"See this nigga to my left? That's my guy right there. The best friend I've ever had. Not a man of a lot of words, but when he speaks . . . he speaks of substance. When he speaks, it means power. See, Saint and I met years ago when I was a senior in college. I had just blown out my knee and didn't know what I was going to do in life. He showed me a new way of thinking. He showed me that I didn't need a lot of friends, just one good one. And I found that in him. My mu'fuckin' partner in crime. We got a lot of money together too. We started a real estate company and haven't looked back since," Zoo said and hesitated as he shot a look over to Saint and winked. Saint smiled, knowing that they hadn't sold one damn house together a day of their lives. Honestly, that was the first time he ever heard something about a real estate company. Saint shook his head in amusement as he tapped Ramina's leg under the table. She chuckled as well, catching on to the inside joke.

"Zoo crazy as hell," Ramina playfully murmured under her breath. She whispered so low that only Saint could hear her. Saint picked up his glass and saluted Zoo, followed by a simple nod. Zoo continued.

"Saint always did right by me and showed me what real friendship is. I tell you all the time, there's not a lot of people that's cut from our cloth. Not too many niggas like us. He told me once that when it comes to friends . . . less is more, so there's plenty of us." Random encouraging shouts from the crowd came from the guests as Zoo's words resonated with them. He was preaching a ghetto sermon.

"I know that's right!" a lady yelled as she clapped her hands.

"Talk to 'em!" another man yelled as if Zoo were in a pulpit.

Zoo paused a moment and picked up his champagne flute. He raised the glass in the air and looked as the waiters continued to do their jobs, not paying him any attention. Then he picked up his speech right where he left off. "I want to wish him and his beautiful wife, Ramina, the best, as they start this new chapter in their lives. I love you both from the bottom of my heart," Zoo said as he dropped his head, signaling that he was done. But he quickly scanned the room and said something in addition.

"And another thing . . . I want to thank the waitstaff for the phenomenal job they're doing tonight. Let's give 'em a round of applause," he said as he motioned for people to clap. The crowd clapped, and a few of the waiters smiled but didn't pay too much attention. They were staying on the task at hand.

"Now, I want everyone to do one more thing for me. Raise your fist like this," Zoo said as he put his fist in the air. People were confused about what exactly he was doing. However, slowly but surely, the guests raised their fists. Zoo looked back at Saint to see if his hand was raised.

Saint just smiled and shook his head. Saint knew that his friend was a charismatic character and sat back and watched the show, not wanting any part of what was about to happen. Once Zoo saw all the hands in the air, he finished off his speech.

"Now stick up your finger like so," he said, as he waved his middle finger in the air. "All these waiters are federal agents, trying to find something out . . . but they won't. We are all law-abiding citizens in this mu'fucka. So, this is a toast to y'all bitch-ass mu'fuckas. Nice try. Spend these good folks' tax money on something that makes a difference," Zoo said with a big smile on his face. The entire room had their middle fingers in the air, and all the attention went on the mostly male waitstaff.

The waiters paused, and their pale white faces all blushed red. There was no denying what Zoo had said. It was the truth. One of the male waiters seemed to be so irate that he couldn't hide it any longer. The 40-something-year-old Caucasian man stood there in shock. He clenched his jaws tightly, and his pale white skin instantaneously turned plum red. It looked like smoke was about to pour out of his ears, he was so hot. Out of pure frustration, he dropped the handful of plates he carried and stormed off. Their cover had been blown, and it seemed almost instantly the other waiters followed suit. The sounds of glasses shattering erupted because multiple "waiters" dropped their plates and walked out. The guests, still with their middle fingers in the air, laughed uncontrollably. They literally laughed the Feds out of the building. It was a beautiful moment.

They say that the Feds have a 98 percent success rate, but on that night, they lost to the streets. It was a historic moment for the bad guys. Saint couldn't do anything but laugh as he shook his head at Zoo. Saint had known about the setup for a little over a month, and rather than complain, he let it play out. The Feds were always trying to find something on him but never could. The recent murder case that he had thrown out made them put him under a microscope. The careful and strategic measures that Saint took to protect himself over the years had all paid off. No paper trail connected him to his empire, and the only blemish he had on his jacket was the murder, and that wasn't even drug related. That incident was personal. He watched as Zoo walked back over to him and took a seat next to him. The DJ played the music again, and everyone talked among themselves at the crazy turn of events. It only added to the legend of Saint. That night was one for the record books.

It was just a few ticks after midnight, and most of the guests were beginning to exit. However, Saint and his wife were still there, enjoying the moment and dancing the night away. They must have had the DJ spin back Lauryn Hill's "Nothing Even Matters" about ten times. The two swayed back and forth as Ramina sang their favorite parts of the song in his ear while snapping her fingers to the snares. Saint's hand was on the small of her back, and her arms hung from his neck as they slowly rocked in perfect unison together. Saint's bow tie was untied, and the first two buttons on his shirt were unbuttoned. He was feeling good as he looked into the eyes of his new wife. Ramina was tipsy, and both of their hearts were full of joy as the thought of their new life had both of them in a blissful, trance-like state. He held a large bottle of champagne in his free hand and smiled at Ramina while gazing deeply into her soul's windows.

"Mi, you're beautiful. You're perfect," he complimented in admiration. He called her "Mi" for short, and she loved it every time she heard it. Her thick frame and wide hips made Saint's mind think about what they were going to do after they left. He looked at her face and admired her skin tone. Her full lips and made-up face were that of perfection like a ghetto Barbie. Baby hairs rested on her edges as her hair lay perfectly. He slid his hand down to her plump backside and cupped her ass, giving it a slight squeeze.

"You always know what to say to make me smile, Saint," Ramina said as she gazed into her husband's slightly red eyes. It made her smile, knowing that he was happy and finally letting loose for a night. He seldom drank, so he was in rare form.

"It's my truth, love. I'm just speaking about what I see. You're the prettiest girl in the world to me. You been here since the beginning, and I appreciate everything. I appreciate your loyalty. For that, I owe you the world," Saint said with sincerity, never breaking eye contact with his lady.

"You're my soul mate, Saint Von Cole," she said as she smiled and looked at her man in admiration.

"You're my soul mate, Ramina Shay Cole," he said, playfully returning the sentiment. They both shared a small laugh and continued to rock.

"Can I ask you a question, mister?" she said.

"Of course, love. Ask me anything," he answered.

"Are you going to leave it alone? Are you done? Like, done-done?"

"Of course," Saint said, as he looked around. "I'm out. There's nothing left for me to do in that world. I'm out," Saint confirmed. He spoke with conviction and was confident in his decision. He was out of the game for good. He saw the skepticism in her face, although she remained silent and nodded her head in contentment. Saint knew that, like everyone else, it was hard to believe.

"I can stay and die, or I can bow out gracefully and live the rest of my life with my best friend. Seems like an easy choice, you hear me?" Saint explained charmingly. He ran his tongue across his top row of teeth and smiled. It was contagious because it instantly made Ramina beam.

She shook her head, blushing.

"What?" Saint asked, wanting to know why she was smiling.

"You always make things so easy. Everything is so easy with you. You never cease to amaze me. You always have an answer to a situation."

Saint pulled her close to his chest and gently kissed her on her forehead. He whispered that he loved her and inhaled deeply as she lay her head on his chest, vibing to the rhythm of the beat and his soul at the same time.

Saint knew that a wise man knows how to make something complicated seem simple. Yet, a fool takes something simple and makes it complicated. Saint understood this, so he moved accordingly. Little did she know, he had been planning his exit for years. Everything that was happening now was a direct result of his strategic thinking. He would always think about a situation in ten different ways before he even told a soul about it, and this instance was no different.

As the song wrapped up, three girls dressed in bridesmaids' gowns approached the newlyweds. The song switched to what the locals called "Bounce" music. Bounce music was legendary in the bayou. The upbeat, fast tempo style was a staple in the culture of New Orleans, and it wasn't a party officially until you had the bounce. The sounds of Big Freedia pumped out of the speakers, and Ramina and her girls all come together while forming a small circle. Saint stepped to the side and smiled, watching his wife have a good time with her girls. That's when he felt the arm of Zoo wrap around him.

"You did it, my nigga," he said just before taking a big gulp from the champagne bottle.

"It feels right," Saint replied as the two stepped off the dance floor, walking side by side.

"Can you believe the fuzz came in this mu'fucka on your wedding day? They will stoop to the lowest of lows to lock a nigga up, won't they?" Zoo said, shaking his head, still in disbelief.

"They can snoop all they want. They ain't got shit on me. Let 'em come. I'm not worried at all," Saint said confidently.

"No doubt . . . No doubt," Zoo replied. He watched as the girls enjoyed themselves and yelled loudly while gyrating their backsides. He loved Ramina's crew because they were all beautiful, young, and rich. They were a power circle, and each one of them had a nice hustle going on. They were infamous throughout the city for being bad girls that loved the bad boys. Ramina was the ringleader of their crew, for sure. She complemented Saint very well by owning one of the most prominent salons in the city, and her online hair store did seven figures each year. Ramina wasn't your typical dope man's wife. She had her own, which made her even more desirable.

Zoo watched closely as the girls moved their big asses in circles in unison and eyed the one he would proposition later. But first, he wanted to talk business with Saint. Saint could turn someone from a small-time hustler into a king with the snap of a finger. Saint was the source of every drug dealer's happiness. He could change their lives with one simple phone call.

"About what you said earlier, I really appreciate that. I been waiting to take my shit to the next level. This is my way to do that," Zoo explained.

"Indeed. Indeed," Saint simply replied.

"I'm expanding," Zoo said, as he stared at nothing in particular. Saint could tell that he was planning his next move. The ambition was pouring out of him. Saint knew that was his best trait, but it also could be his worst.

"Expanding, huh?" Saint said.

"Yeah, I'm going to shoot back home and set up shop in Flint. I have a few cats out there that's moving around. They just need a steady pipeline to feed their people, feel me?" Zoo explained.

"After I get back from the honeymoon, we are on the first thing smoking to Cuba," Saint assured him.

"Cubana," Zoo said as he did a bad interpretation of a Spanish accent. He continued, "Oh yeah, I need you to plug me with homegirl too. You know . . . your witch doctor out there. I need that shit on my side, just in case shit goes left. I still can't believe that case got dropped. No trial—not nothing. Whatever you paid that woman . . . It was worth it."

"Was it worth it?" Saint asked. He was asking himself that question, more so than Zoo. "And she's not a witch doctor," Saint said as he shook his head at his friend's misconception. "It's not that simple. There's more to it than just voodoo dolls and that bullshit you see in movies," Saint said, as he had mental flashes of the things he saw on his last trip. He had been there plenty of times before, but that last time, things were definitely different.

Chapter Two

Monkey on the Back

Bums and dope fiends were scattered in various huddles under the overpass. It was in the wee hours of the night when only the street zombies and hustlers were up with their own personal agendas. A congregation spot for the city's have-nots, homeless, and druggies was under the city bridge. Two different bonfires inside old aluminum trash cans were ablaze, also known as a poor man's heating system. As the small fires illuminated the dark area, bums circled them, waving their hands over the flames in an attempt to keep warm. The scene resembled Hades with how fires danced in the air, and soulless addicts wandered aimlessly. Some of them looked like statues that leaned to the side from the effects of the heroin's potency.

Tay had become a familiar face on the scene over the past few months. She was by far the youngest fiend on the scene. Earlier, she had left the church, which was only a block away. She slumped on the soiled sofa as she could barely keep her eyes open. She dazedly moaned as she tried to sit upright but flopped back because her upper torso felt as if it weighed a ton. She immediately melted back into the couch after her failed attempt.

She felt wetness in between her thighs and looked down to see a huge wet spot in her crotch area. She groggily woke up completely from her heroin-induced nod and realized that she had pissed herself. This was a common thing among junkies. The rush that an addict felt when the drugs traveled through their veins was described as orgasmic. The sensation was like no other and sometimes caused the urge to relieve yourself. Tay had taken the money that Gunner had given her at the wedding and went straight to the dope man for her fix. Before that day, she had been clean for an entire week. However, seeing Ramina walk down the aisle to Saint pushed her to try to numb the pain. She just wanted the pain in her heart to go away, and the only way she knew to do that was to get high.

She gathered herself and stood up. She straightened her jacket and rubbed her frazzled hair. She looked around and noticed the familiar faces under the bridge and felt a sharp pain shoot through her stomach. She doubled over in pain and vomited onto the pavement. She knew her body was about to become dope sick. She was on a countdown to being in unbearable pain if she didn't get another shot of dope in her veins. The small fix that she had gotten earlier wasn't enough to keep her from going through the motions of being ill.

Her eyes scanned her surroundings, then focused on the gas station across the street. She headed that way to see if she could catch a young hustler to try to make a trade. "A trade" was a term in the streets when fiends would trade sexual favors for drugs, and Tay was open to it all. She would do anything to get the monkey off her back and prevent herself from getting sick.

She made her way across the street, where two guys stood outside of the station with hoodies on. She crossed her arms and hugged herself tightly as she made her way over to them.

***

Saint opened the door to his black Range Rover and watched as his newly wedded wife stepped in. They were just outside of the reception hall that was near the church where they were just married. As he took a swallow of the champagne that was in his hand, he studied his wife closely, admiring her. He gulped the bottle and wiped his mouth as he swallowed. He then walked around the car and hopped into the driver's seat, but not before pulling off his blazer and placing it across the middle armrest. A packet of bad dope fell from his pocket and onto Ramina's lap. Ramina wasn't green to the game, so she immediately knew what it was. She picked it up and examined it.

"This looks different. This isn't Cubana," she said confidently as she examined the altered stamp.

"I know, I know. It's some fake shit going around, and I have to get to the bottom of it," Saint said as he placed his hand on the steering wheel.

"I thought you were out, Saint," Ramina said as a brief wave of disappointment was written all over her face.

"I know, love. I just want to get to the bottom of it before Zoo starts shooting up shit. You know how he is," Saint expounded.

"Yea, I know, but that's not your concern anymore. You promised that this was over, babe. You promised," Ramina pleaded.

"You know what? You're right," Saint admitted, knowing that if he didn't just walk away from the game, something would always pull him back in. Instantly, Ramina smiled like a young schoolgirl.

"Well, I'll get rid of this for you. I'm going to make sure you leave this shit alone. We are about to start our new life together. We're leaving the bayou for good. So it can just be us two," she said joyfully. She tucked the pack in her purse to ensure that Saint wouldn't follow up on the street issue.

He watched as Ramina immediately took off her Louboutin stiletto heels and rested her feet on the white carpet of his car. They caught each other's eyes and smiled, both thinking the same thing. They couldn't wait to reach their home so they could make love for the first time as husband and wife. The sexual tension had been building up all night, and they were lusting after each other. He watched as Ramina giggled and worked her dress up, exposing her bald vagina. She pressed her back against her door so that she was completely facing him. She put one of her legs on the dash so that he could get a perfect view of her love box. Her big, brown legs always turned Saint on as he smirked at her voluptuous physique. She spread her legs apart as far as she could and rested her head on the window. Saint slowly pulled off.

He looked over in awe and smiled as he watched as she gave him a show. She sexily put her fingers in her mouth and made sure that she put enough saliva on them to do the job. She then circled her tongue around her own fingers, dropping them down to her box.

"Oooh," she purred. The moment her wet fingers reached her clitoris, it pulsated. Ramina smiled in pleasure as she felt the heartbeat in her love box. She tenderly tapped her vagina, causing a loud, wet sound to erupt. With every tap, it seemed as if her button grew and grew, slightly peeking from her lips. She continued to moan, all while keeping eye contact with Saint. She then applied pressure to herself and slowly stroke herself in slow, circular motions. Saint tried his best to focus on the road, but it was hard to stay on track. His eyes went back and forth from the road to his girl. He felt his manhood begin to grow. He thought about how he would bend her over as soon as they walked through their door. Ramina took her foot and placed it on Saint's crotch, searching for his growing tool. Her foot stopped when she found it, and that's when her mouth watered.

"Yeah, I'm livin' like that," Saint said playfully in a deep New Orleans accent, showing off his girth and strength. His bottom row of golds was on full display as he ran his tongue across his white top row. She wanted to taste him and took it as a personal challenge to make him erupt before they reached home. She got on her knees, in the seat, and unbuckled his belt buckle. She frantically searched for his rod, and when she found it, she let out a satisfying moan. Saint leaned back his seat slightly while keeping one hand on the steering wheel. He lifted his shirt so he could get a clear view of what was about to happen. He watched as Ramina wrapped her full lips around him, slowly swirling her tongue around his tip before swallowing him whole. She slowly made him disappear and reappear, working her magic. The slurping sounds made the experience even more enticing for Saint as he let out an unintentional moan. She wiggled her ass in the air as she pleased him, and the sight made Saint even stronger.

As Ramina pleased him, a bell sounded. Saint's eyes drifted to the speedometer, and he saw that he had low fuel.

"Damn, love, I gotta get some gas," he whispered, and he stared at the needle, pointing to "E." He watched as she slowly bobbed her head up and down, licking the sides of his shaft just before devouring the whole thing. He peeked at the huge BP sign and decided to make a quick stop before they were left stranded on the side of the road because of an empty gas tank. As he whipped into the gas station, he tapped Ramina so she could pause their session.

"Um," she hummed as she popped his tool out of her mouth. She sat up and wiped her mouth as she looked around to make sure no one was watching. They both looked at each other and burst into laughter. "Nigga, hurry up," she said playfully.

"Yes, ma'am," he answered as he made himself decent before exiting the car. He had on his dress slacks and an open shirt, displaying his tattooed belly and designer belt. His Valentino loafers clicked the pavement with each step. As he approached the store to pay for his gas, he saw a few youngsters standing by the door. He didn't know them, but obviously, they knew who he was because before he could reach the door, one of them opened it for him.

"Respect . . ." Saint greeted as he nodded to the youngsters, making sure he made eye contact with both of them before stepping through the threshold.

When Saint made it into the store, the young man that held the door open looked over at his partner with concerned eyes. He knew who Saint was and his prominent position in the streets. Saint was the plug, and every young hustler wanted to get put into position by him. Not a lot of people knew who Saint was, but if you knew . . . you knew. Saint could change a life with the snap of his fingers, so when the young dealers saw him, he was like a real-life walking lottery ticket. They just hoped that they were lucky enough to get on his radar . . . lucky enough to be a part of Saint's team. In the streets, he was a god.

However, the thought of what was going on in the alley just a few feet away was causing concern for them. They prayed to the heavens that Saint didn't notice what they knew. One of their partners was having his way with Tay in the dirty alley. It was well known that Tay was Saint's loved one, and no one wanted to be on the opposite of Saint's wrath over her—nobody.

***

"Move your hands," the young man said harshly as he looked down at Tay. Tay was on her knees in the wet alley.

Tears were in her eyes as she took the young boy into her mouth. She felt ashamed and embarrassed, knowing she was pleasing a 16-year-old boy just to get her next fix. The young hustler had his eyes on Tay for years and never thought that he would have her in the position that she was in now. The pimply-faced teen was as black as tar, and his demented, gap-toothed smile was on display. His skinny jeans were wrapped around his ankles, and he trapped the bottom of his shirt between his chin and chest to get a clear view. His big belly hung freely as he watched his manhood disappear and reappear from the blow job. His lustful eyes were fixated on the Cuban beauty that sucked him off. Her wavy hair was something he yearned after, and it made the experience even that more exhilarating to him. He couldn't believe he had Tay blowing him. She, at one time, was the catch of the neighborhood. Her association with Saint and Zoo made her a hood trophy, a notch under his belt.

He was having the time of his life, but Tay felt disgusting. As she slurped on the fat, young thug, a wave of shame overcame her. But then the pain in her stomach reminded her of why she was doing what she was doing. She felt the cold concrete and wetness on her knees and wanted it just to be over and done with. Another sharp pain hit her once again, but this time it was much more painful. It was so painful that she grimaced, causing her to scrape her teeth across the young thug's shaft. She jerked back and shrieked in discomfort.

"Bitch, watch your teeth," he said through his clenched teeth. He frowned and stepped back, snatching his tool from Tay's mouth. She dropped her head down in humiliation as she wiped the excessive saliva from around her mouth.

"Sorry," she whispered as she tried to grab his penis once again. He aggressively slapped her hand away. He then grabbed her forcefully by her face and made her look at him.

"Don't be sorry . . . be careful," he said with a demented look in his eyes.

Tay nodded her head in understanding and then gingerly took him into her mouth again. She worked her mouth on him, hoping that he would climax soon so she could get her fix from him. He threw his head back in pleasure as he gripped the back of her head and rammed himself into her mouth. She gagged and almost threw up because he was hitting her tonsils. He held her head and went as deep as he could, blocking her airwaves as he felt himself about to explode inside of her mouth. She placed her hands on his thighs and tried to push away so she could get air, but that's when he just held her tighter while releasing himself.

"Aaaagh," he moaned as a walnut-sized glob shot into the back of her throat. He finally released his grip on her head and stepped back, shaking his tool off as the semen flung from his penis.

Tay gagged and heaved as she tried her best to catch her breath. She fell to the ground, feeling dizzy from the lack of oxygen. Tay held her chest and panted heavily as she was now on all fours like a dog, searching for air. The young hustler put his tool inside of his jeans and laughed as he saw Tay suffer just beneath him. The sight of her gagging only fed into his ego. He wasn't a good-looking guy by any means. In his mind, it was payback for all the pretty girls that dissed him throughout his life. Somehow, treating her like shit made him feel better about the rejection.

He reached into his pocket and pulled out a small pack of heroin. He tossed it on the ground. It landed just to the right of Tay. She hurried and scooped it up, yearning to feel its power rush through her veins.

The hustler walked away so that he could boast to his friends about dogging the beauty. But before he could clear the alley, he heard her voice.

"Hey! Hey! What the fuck is this, man?" Tay yelled as she stood to her feet, examining the bag.

"It's what the fuck I gave you," the young man said as he paused and looked back at her.

"Yo, what's up with you? We had a deal. This isn't a forty pack," Tay yelled in disappointment as she rushed over to him and grabbed him by his jacket. He quickly snatched away and spat in her face. He had given her a small pack that he used to provide samples to the fiends. It wasn't enough to satisfy the intense hunger of a seasoned junkie. He had planned to short her from the jump, assuming she would just be happy with what he had given her.

"What the fuck?" she yelled again, as she wiped the spit from her forehead. The hustler walked away, leaving her there dumbfounded. He returned to post up right in front of the store, where his friends were waiting.

As the young man posted up, he saw the look on his friends' faces and immediately knew something was wrong.

"Fuck wrong wit' y'all?" he asked, looking back and forth between the two guys.

But before they could answer, Saint came out of the store. As he walked out, Tay was coming from around the corner in a rage. She was about to curse the hustler out but seeing Saint made her freeze up and become speechless. She stopped dead in her tracks and looked at the only man she ever truly loved. Saint was speechless as well. He froze when he saw his "baby." Although he didn't have the same type of attraction to her that she had for him, he did truly love her. He had more of a big brother feeling for her, and seeing her in her current state broke his heart into tiny little pieces. He looked at her eyes and knew that she had been using. The way they were sunk in and the dark circles were a dead giveaway that she was on the hunt for a fix.

Saint opened his mouth to speak, but nothing came out. He was watching his little baby tweaking, and it killed him. Tay could feel the awkwardness and just wanted to run away in pure disgrace. However, the pains in her stomach made her brush past him and approach the guy that had shorted her. Saint watched as she flew past him, and his eyes followed her as she stood in front of the group of guys. Saint took a deep breath and headed to his car and pumped the gas.

Damn, she looks so bad. Li'l baby don't even look like herself, he thought to himself, referring to her as a name he used to call her. He gave her that name because she was so tiny. Although she was 20, she had the body of a little boy. She had very small breasts and wasn't curvy at all. However, her pure beauty overcompensated for her lack of voluptuousness. Tay was his little baby, and that title had so many layers that only they understood.

He shook his head as if he were trying to shake off the concern that he had for her. But it didn't work. That love was embedded deep in his heart, and no matter how he tried to dismiss it, he couldn't. He glanced back and tried to see what was going on. He saw that they were arguing, but he knew that he couldn't get into another person's street business. He could tell in her eyes that she was fighting inner demons, and this crushed him to the core.

As he pumped the gas, he kept wanting to go and just save her, but he knew it was too late. His name was too good in the streets to break the code of it. He couldn't see himself trying to save a mere dope fiend from some petty business that wasn't his own. No matter how he cut it, it would seem as if he were being a square if he intervened.

He hopped back into the car. Ramina was sipping on the bottle of champagne and jamming to the music that she had turned up. The sounds of his speakers knocked as smooth R&B music sounded. The chill ambiance of Summer Walker's song had her in her element. She swayed back and forth with her eyes closed while snapping her fingers to the beat. She was oblivious to what was going on outside of the car and was in her own world. Saint hopped in with a heavy heart. He wanted to tell Ramina about what he saw, but he knew that it was a tender topic, so he decided to keep it to himself. He gave her a half smile and put the car in drive just before pulling off. Ramina finished off the bottle and looked over to Saint with bedroom eyes. She now wanted to finish what she had started as she looked down at his pelvic area.

"Let me get you together, babe," she said as she tossed the empty bottle in the back and then leaned forward. She licked her lips as she unbuckled his pants once again. She pulled his slightly erect tool out and circled his tip with her tongue. She knew from experience that had always got him to stand straight up in no time.

Saint drove and tried to focus on what Ramina was doing to him, but his mind was on Tay. He glanced in the rearview mirror, trying to see her, but they had gotten too far down the road. He thought that she was out of his system, but the connection was obviously still there. The look in her eyes . . . He couldn't shake those eyes. Those pretty eyes and the hurt behind them tugged at his heart. *Where did I go wrong with li'l baby? It wasn't supposed to be like this,* he thought as the guilt mixed in with heartbreak and played with his emotions. His mind drifted, and he replayed all the scenarios where he could have done something differently. As Ramina continued to work on him below, the heaviness of his heart pushed water out of his eyes. He couldn't understand why the girl's soul was tied to his like it was. No matter how hard he wanted to let her go, he just couldn't. He felt responsible for Tay's happiness, and anything beneath that felt like a failure on his part.

Ramina abruptly stopped and sat up. She looked over at Saint to see what was wrong with him. He had gone soft, and that was never a problem for him. He stood tall every single time, and his dick would get hard if she so much as touched it. But she knew what was wrong. It was written all over her man's face, and the water in his eyes was a clear indication of what she already knew. She crossed her arms as she looked straightforward, her mind churning as conflict manifested in her soul.

"Go get her," Ramina said reluctantly. She had seen Tay when they pulled up and saw their interaction as well. She decided to pretend that she didn't see it, not wanting to ruin her wedding day. But it was evident that something was bothering Saint. Ramina loved him so much that she was willing to hurt so he could be happy. Saving Tay would make him happy, and Ramina had accepted that. She knew the love that he had for Tay and seeing his pain really did something to her.

"What?" Saint said as he put his tool back in his pants. He looked at her, confused. It was as if she were reading his mind.

"You heard me. Go get your li'l baby," she said as she looked over at him, leaned forward, and gently cupped his face. "I understand. Go back," she whispered.

"I'm so sorry, love," Saint said, as he looked into his wife's eyes. A single tear slid down his face, and it simply broke Ramina's heart. She felt water build up in her eyes as the sorrow in her chest created a feeling of anxiety.

"It's fine. Turn around," she whispered, as she sat back in her seat and looked away just as the tear fell . . . just in time so that Saint didn't notice. He quickly hit a U-turn and headed back to the gas station to rescue Tay.

"You betta get outta my mu'fuckin' face. Take that pack and handle your business. You lucky I gave you what I gave you for that whack-ass head you gave me," the fat thug said as he looked at Tay with disgust. She had been begging him for the past five minutes, and he was growing agitated by her audacity.

"That's not fair. Now, give me what you owe," Tay said with pure rage as she balled up her fists and tears fell from her eyes. She knew that she would be in for a night of pain if she didn't get enough to keep the monkey off her back. What he had given her wasn't going to cut it. She needed more dope. She needed it bad and would do anything to get it.

"I'll do whatever you want me to do. Just please give me enough to shake this pain," Tay begged as an intense pain shot through her stomach once again.

The fat thug seemed as if Tay's agony amused him. He was about to push her away, but he got an idea when he saw the desperation in her eyes.

"Let my boys hit it. If you let all of us hit that pussy, you can have this," he said as he dug into his pocket and pulled out a pack. Instantly, Tay cried harder, knowing that she couldn't oblige to his request.

"I'm sorry, I can't do that," she said as she dropped to her knees in shame and teared up.

"This nasty bitch on her period," the fat thug said as he looked at his boys and laughed.

"That mouth still work, though," one of the other boys suggested.

"You damn right. That mouth works just fine," the fat thug said as he smirked and grabbed his junk and rubbed it through his jeans, thinking about the round two of action he was about to get.

"Okay, I will suck off all three of y'all. Just give me the dope first, so I know you're serious," Tay pleaded as she looked up with her hands clasped in a praying position. The fat thug reached into his pocket and pulled out a forty pack. He then tossed it on the ground where Tay was kneeling. She hurriedly scooped up the pack and it put it in her pocket.

"Come on," she said as she wiped away her tears and headed toward the alley.

The boys childishly chuckled and followed her into the darkness.

"I'm first, my nigga," one of the boys yelled as he pulled out his semi-erect penis and walked over to Tay, who was already on her knees. They didn't even notice the Range Rover pull up a few yards away. Saint smoothly stepped out and approached the alley. The sound of his calm, deep voice sounded.

"Show is over," Saint calmly said as he brushed past the two waiting thugs and headed over to Tay and the guy that she was about blow. He grabbed Tay by the arm and forcefully lifted her to her feet.

"Saint, let me go!" Tay yelled as she thought about getting her fix over anything else. Saint gave Tay a stern look as he gripped her tighter and pulled her close. She quickly backed down, knowing that Saint wasn't someone to play with. He had the savage look of a lion in his eyes, and it instantly sent chills down Tay's spine. After a few seconds of silence, Saint guided her past the crew and toward his car.

"Nigga trying to save the bitch. She belongs to the streets, my nigga," the fat thug said playfully while Saint's back was turned. The two other boys were shocked that he said something sideways to Saint. Their eyes grew as big as golf balls by their comrade's remark. One of the boys even tapped the fat thug and whispered, "What the fuck, man?" They understood who Saint was, but obviously, their friend didn't.

Saint heard what was said as he put Tay in the backseat. He remained quiet until he got her inside secure and shut the door. Then he calmly turned around and slid his hands in his pockets. He slowly walked over to the group of boys with a slight smile.

"What's your name?" Saint asked as he approached the fat one.

"I'm Fatboy," the guy proudly said as he poked his chest out a tad bit more than it already was.

"You know who I am?" Saint asked as he stepped closer to Fatboy, chest to chest.

"Nah, not really. *Should* I know?" Fatboy asked sarcastically.

"I know," one of the other boys said as he nervously raised his hand. They knew Fatboy wasn't aware of who Saint was. He had been locked up for the past few summers. Saint quickly put his finger to his lips, signaling that the boy should be quiet.

"My name is Saint. I didn't mean any disrespect, li'l nigga. This business is personal and—"

"Li'l nigga?" Fatboy said, cutting Saint off. He looked around at his boys like he couldn't believe what was said to him. He slid his hand into his back pocket and grabbed the small .25-caliber pistol out and transferred it into his front pocket. He intentionally wanted Saint to see what he had. He then continued. "I'm big weight out here. I advise you to take yo' ass where you came from. What you, a deacon or something?" he asked as he looked Saint up and down and saw his attire, not knowing that it was his wedding day.

"Nah, beloved. I'm no deacon. But check this out . . . You got it. You won. I apologize for the misunderstanding," Saint said politely, as he slowly put his hand on Fatboy's shoulder and patted it one time. "Have a good night, gentlemen," Saint said without one bit of malice or aggressiveness in his tone. He simply just patted the boy's shoulder and turned to walk away. He looked over to his left and saw Zoo creeping from their blind side. He didn't even bother to look over directly at Zoo. It was business as usual for them. Minutes before, Saint had called him and told him what was going down with Tay. Zoo had been parked on the side, watching the whole thing play out.

As Saint got to his car door, Zoo was preparing to blow Fatboy's brains out. Zoo knew exactly who to hit because of the discreet signal that Saint had given him by merely tapping the shoulder of Fatboy. He was nonverbally giving Zoo the greenlight. As Saint drove off, a loud thud rang off in the distance. It was the sound of a single gunshot that resonated, echoing through the air. Saint and Ramina didn't flinch at the noise, already knowing the cause of it. Tay jumped, frightened, and tried to see what was going on, but Saint had already pulled out of the lot and out of eyeshot of the homicide. In the streets, Saint was feared, and his reputation was something that he would guard with his life. Too bad Fatboy didn't know any better. He would now have to find out about who Saint was on the *other* side . . . because he was clueless in this realm.

Chapter Three

Toad You

Ramina cried a cascade of tears as she sped down the highway, pushing nearly eighty miles per hour. The top was dropped as she glided in and out of lanes on the interstate. She needed to feel the force of the wind. She wanted to *feel* it. She had to feel something . . . something other than what she was feeling on that early morning. Everything was just so heavy on her soul, heavier than anything had ever been. Her entire being was shaken, and everything that she knew was for certain somehow was now unreliable. The picture-perfect life that she finally thought she had seemed to be snatched from under her. The only man that she truly loved was in love with someone else. She could tell. She just knew. There was something about seeing those tears in Saint's eyes that told her the truth. Not his words or his actions, but those tears told her everything that she *didn't* want to know. She had been with him for years and never once saw tears from that man.

Ramina had no makeup on her face, and her natural brown skin glowed in the sunlight. Being in public like this was a rarity for her. She hadn't walked out of the house in years without being dolled up. But on this day, she just had to get away from the anguish that was back home.

She slightly raised her oversized sunglasses with her index finger and wiped tears away as she wept. She cried uncontrollably as she thought about how her husband was at home tending to that dope-sick woman, rather than celebrating their new marriage with her. The loud purr from her silver Porsche Panamera ripped through the airwaves. She neared one hundred miles per hour. The sounds of Lauryn Hill knocked through her sound system as her long, jet-black hair blew wildly in the air.

She was supposed to be on an airplane on her way to Italy for her honeymoon. Instead, she was in still in the bayou . . . heartbroken. She was there wondering if she had made a mistake by marrying Saint. *How can he be trying to put her together, while I'm fucking falling apart?* she thought as the tears continued to flow. She had loved Saint with every morsel in her body, and she knew he was a good man. The problem was that he was being a good man to someone else. Anxiety crept in. Although she tried to breathe slowly, the heartache was overweighing it all.

"Why does he love her? I fucking hate her. I *hate* that bitch. I wish she would just die," Ramina cried as she smashed the accelerator to the floor, pushing the luxury vehicle to the limit. She was now nearing one hundred twenty miles per hour. Somehow, the speed seemed to help her release the unwanted tension that had built up inside of her.

Ramina's disappointment and frustration had reached its boiling point. She felt like she was being robbed—robbed of the life that she had deserved. She stood by Saint's side and played her position the right way throughout the years. The pain slowly started to become rage. She possessed a massive flame that burned deep within her soul, all behind the man that the streets feared, and the ladies lusted after. She was drawn to his quiet power. She was addicted to him, and she wasn't going to let him go.

"Fuck that!" she yelled as she squeezed the steering wheel as tightly as her grips would allow. She let out a roar of passion that she never knew she had.

"Aaaagh!" she screamed, which turned into a gut-wrenching sob. She angrily hit her steering wheel. She wasn't a hateful person, but over that man, she would become the worst. He was her trigger. *He was her trigger*.

She felt something in the pit of her stomach rumble as nausea set in. Suddenly, the urge to throw up overwhelmed her. She was sweating profusely and dry heaving while becoming dizzy. Vomit came up in her mouth. She leaned over to spit the vomit out in her passenger seat. Her eyes grew as big as golf balls when she saw all the clear secretions that she had thrown up. But it wasn't the spit and secretions that alerted her. It was the small green frog hopping around in it, struggling to escape the thick liquid . . .

What the fuck? she thought as she tried to refocus her fuzzy vision. Her heart raced rapidly. She was confused and frightened at the same time. She shook her head and focused on the road . . . but it was too late.

The sound of a thunderous crash resonated in the air, followed by screeching tires and crushing metal. Ramina crashed her car into the back of an eighteen-wheeler semitruck, instantly propelling her body into the air like a rag doll. She was launched about fifty yards and crashed violently onto the pavement. Her body rolled over a dozen times against the concrete, ripping her flesh with each flip. It all happened so fast . . . She never saw it coming. She didn't have a chance. As Ramina lay there slipping in and out of consciousness, she was completely bloodied, and the left side of her face was skinned from skidding on the road. She tried to move, but she couldn't. The broken bones and trauma wouldn't allow her to.

She felt her life slip away, and all she could think about was Saint. She just wanted him to come and save her. She wanted him to make sure that she would make it through. Her thoughts went to Tay. Her eyes were getting heavy as her vision got blurry, and she saw an animal standing over her. She was horrified, yet she could not gasp, scream, or move. She was just there. It looked like a monkey, but she wasn't sure. She couldn't really make it out clearly. She thought that it was odd. She had never seen that type of animal up close other than in zoos, and that was behind glass. Ramina took a deep breath as her eyes slowly closed. She couldn't fight the urge to sleep . . . So she let go.

Saint sat in the chair next to the bedside of Tay. He watched closely as Tay scratched her body vigorously and fidgeted in her sleep. Her body was drenched in sweat as if a bucket of water had been dumped on her. She faintly whimpered, and she continually clawed at herself. She scratched so hard that she drew blood, making thick welts on her arms and neck, and trickles of blood were in different spots on the white sheets. Saint understood what was happening to Tay and knew there was nothing he could do about it, but just wait it out. Her body was going through withdrawals, and it yearned for the drug that made Saint wealthy. Saint was sitting in a chair right next to the bed and watched, knowing that he was helpless, and that's what broke his heart. He wasn't that much older than Tay, but in a way, he felt like she was his little baby. He felt the responsibility of taking care of her, no matter how difficult it was.

Something deep inside was telling him that he was doing the right thing. He rubbed her hair, gently laying it down and brushing it in one direction. He could feel the wetness from the sweat, but he didn't care. He just wanted her to get better. He slowly caressed her and whispered to her. "Shhh . . . shhh," he said, trying to comfort her, and instantly he noticed the murmurs slowed, and her body got more relaxed. "That's my girl," he whispered as he leaned over and tenderly kissed her forehead. He continued to rub her until she stopped tweaking altogether. He half-grinned while watching her closely. He knew that she was a diamond in the rough and had the potential to be something great. However, her past demons had a hold on her, a strong one. She had been through so much in her life, and he knew that if he didn't help her, no one else would. At 21, she had suffered three lifetime's worth of pain and despair. Her pure beauty hid her pain well, and she looked nothing like what she had been through.

His thoughts drifted to his new wife, and guilt set in. The thought of him asking her to go through this at the time of their wedding really bothered him. He felt selfish, knowing that he temporarily ignored her feelings to tend to Tay, who had a hold on him, and he could not understand why. He thought that he was the cause of her current struggle, so, therefore, he felt responsible for her. He hadn't seen her in over a year, but there wasn't a day that passed that he didn't think of her. When he saw her in that alley, he felt God was giving him a second chance to right his wrongs with her.

Although he had her blessings to help Tay, he knew deep inside that Mi had put his feelings before her own. He was so worried about Tay that he never thought about how Mi must've felt. He understood that she hadn't deserved to be anyone's second option or on a back burner.

He felt a flutter in his heart as if he just saw Ramina's face. He shook his head, ashamed of himself, and headed out of the room to tell her he was sorry. He hadn't even realized he had been in the guest room with Tay all night. Not until he saw the rays of the sunlight peeking from the living room blinds did he notice that he had broken day while tending to her.

He walked across his spacious home, and it felt unusually cold. The ten thousand-square foot estate was one that Mi had made their home. Her woman's touch shined through the exquisite interior design. Her stellar creativity was one of the many things he loved about her. It was simply beautiful. Saint walked across the marble floors and looked up at the high ceiling. Beautiful baby saints were hand drawn on his ceilings. He was amazed every time he looked at it. It was Ramina's idea, and it added character to the home. It was like their mini Vatican with beautiful brown faces rather than pale ones. He reached the porcelain wraparound stairs that led to the second floor and headed toward their bedroom.

When he walked in, he expected to see Ramina in the mirror, doing her hair and makeup as she did every morning. He entered, ready to apologize for his actions, but he found himself standing there alone. The bed was perfectly made up, and the room was empty. A small note was on the bed with her handwriting on it. Just next to the note were two first-class tickets to Italy. As he read through the paper, tears formed in his eyes, but none fell. Her words seemed to talk directly to his heart. He dropped his head and thought back to how it all began. He thought about how times had changed over the past few years. He sat on the bed and just stared at the paper in disbelief. At the time, he thought that it was the beginning of a new chapter in his life. Now, looking back, he realized it was a part of the ending. He wished he had never been opened to the things that Cuba offered.

He sat on the bed and thought deeply. He remembered when things were so simple, and life seemed easy. He looked to his left and saw a Bible there. It had a sticky note with Ramina's handwriting on it. It simply read,

Give this to her . . . Matthew 11:28–30

He grabbed the Bible, stood up, and walked back to the room where Tay was. She was still in there fighting her demons and sweating profusely as she slept in obvious agony. There was an onslaught of moaning and scratching as she clawed and dug into her own skin. It was hard for Saint to watch, but he knew that she had to go through the withdrawal process to get better eventually.

He wanted to run out and find Ramina, though he knew that Tay really needed him. He was torn. Deep down in his soul, he recognized that the right thing to do was to go after his newly wedded wife. But what about Tay? What was she supposed to do without any help? She had no one in the entire world except him.

Saint looked at his li'l baby in pain, and it shook him to his core. At that moment, he realized that he truly loved her. It was because of the way she made him feel and the emotion that she pulled out of him. It wasn't a romantic relationship at all . . . Well, not in Saint's eyes. It was a complicated love between those two. Deep in his heart, he felt that he was responsible for her happiness. That was a heavy burden for anyone to have, but he knew that he owned it. He could not wrap his mind around his bond with her. It felt as if he were rooted to this girl. From the surface, it appeared as if it were a brother/sister relationship, but from Saint's point of view, he wanted to protect her as if she were his daughter. But the truth was, Tay looked at him as more than that. She was deeply in love with him, and he realized that. That's why the relationship was so toxic. His mind drifted back to the first time he met her in Cuba. It was the night that his life changed forever.

Chapter Four

Lion and Water

Two Years Before . . .

The sun was just rising, and the orange and purple hues blended perfectly on the sky's horizon. Blue water from the waves washed up on the shore and wet the entire backside of Ramina. She lay on the edge of the beach shore, just close enough to feel the water wash up. She wore a sheer cover-up robe that left nothing for the imagination. Her wide hips were on full display as she parted her thick brown thighs. Saint lay naked, right in between her legs, kissing her gently. Her red, pedicured toes were dangling in the air as she gripped the sand while gasping for air.

Ramina arched her back and moaned as Saint slowly rocked in and out of her cleanly shaven love box. He took his time, as usual, rocking back and forth, making sure he stayed deep inside of her while doing so. Ramina couldn't help to be in love. The man that was making love to her was her soul mate. Everything about Saint was perfect for her liking. His size, his girth, and his rhythm were tailor-made. It seemed as if he had been specially made for her. She loved the way he made love to her. He was never loud, he never went fast, and he was never weak. She could feel his power in each and every stroke . . . every time. She loved the weight that he put on her when they were intimate. For some odd reason, it comforted her and made her feel safe. As Saint rocked back and forth, he placed his lips by her left earlobe and whispered everything he wanted her to know. Saint was skilled and seasoned enough to know that anything you wanted to stick in a woman's thoughts had to be said during sex . . . good sex, that is. It was seduction at its highest level.

"You are my soul mate," he said in his deep baritone as the sound of the ocean echoed through the air. It was a perfect combination, his voice and nature's ambiance. Earlier that morning, he had wakened her up with kisses and, shortly after, walked her to the beach. They were just outside a private villa in Aruba. It sat directly on the beach, and Saint took full advantage of the majestic layout. He wanted to celebrate her birthday correctly, so he took her international to hail her special day. Saint and Ramina had traveled the world together and made love on different beaches around the globe. It was "their thing." They traveled several times a year and lived life to the fullest. They had been together since they were teens, and they deserved it . . . They deserved each other. Their passports were stamped up and barely had room for any more.

He gently lifted off her so that he was looking her directly into her eyes. He stretched out his arms, flexing his muscles as he repositioned himself while remaining deep inside, touching her bottom. He continued stroking her with a slow, constant pace . . . making sure he stayed at the back of her love box. He was applying that pressure, that heaviness that kept her clitoris engaged. Ramina stared at him intensely and thought about all the reasons why she was so in love with her man . . . her lion. She loved the way his full beard hung like a mane. His belly slightly poked out, but as she glanced down, she could still see him sliding in and out of her. Saint gradually changed pace, giving her longer strokes. She grabbed the back of his neck and raised her knees, pulling them back closer to her chest, thus, giving him more access to her.

She mouthed, "I love you," as a tear rolled down her face, feeling overwhelmed by his pure love and energy. Saint was just different. She had never cried while making love before she met Saint, but with him, it happened almost every time. They were not tears of pain, discomfort, or even of the slightest sorrow. She cried because she was elated. She cried because she knew that he loved her without any bias. His love was unwavering, intentional, and most of all, it was unconditional. The way he looked at her while he sexed her was almost hypnotizing. He never looked away or was embarrassed. The constant eye contact made it more dreamlike. He stared at her while slowly tapping her. This was a nonverbal language that gave her a sense of security. His confidence gave her strength, and this exchanging of energy always was food for her soul.

"Saint, I love you so much. You . . . You feel so good, baby," she moaned as the tears steadily flowed. She smiled while biting her bottom lip in pleasure. Saint's constant stroking and patience were about to pay off. He had been building up her climax for the past twenty-five minutes, and she could feel her release nearing. She adored the way he handled her. He was never rough with her; always patient.

Saint stared into his woman's eyes, and the way her breathing became rapid, he knew she was about to reach her orgasm. He ran his tongue across his lips as he felt his tool get even more erect. The sight of her curvy body and big breasts turned him on. Her dark areoles were huge, and he saw them beginning to get erect as well. He loved the way they jiggled with every thrust. He listened carefully as she whispered in between gasps.

"I'm about to come . . . I'm about to come. Don't stop. Please, don't stop," she said as she gripped his forearms and dug her nails into them.

Saint wasn't a rookie by any means, so he stayed the course and didn't change up his rhythm. Through experience, he knew that when a woman tells you she is about to have an orgasm, the last thing you do is speed up. That was a novice mistake that most men made. They had no patience. Saint had plenty. He didn't do anything fast. He understood that you should keep the same speed and stay at the same spot when a woman is reaching her boiling point. So that's exactly what he did. He steadily glided in and out of her until he felt her vagina walls contract and get tight around his pole. Ramina's body jerked violently, and that's when he knew she was there. He slid his pole out of her and tapped her clitoris swiftly with his tip. After a few hard taps, a geyser of liquid shot from her box and crashed against Saint's stomach.

"Aaaagh," she yelled loudly as she let herself go, squirting everywhere. The wet sensation made Saint explode as well. He shot his load on her belly as her final squirts seeped out. They had climaxed together and found themselves on their backs, looking at the sun come out. It was a beautiful thing. It was perfect timing.

"Happy birthday, pretty girl," Saint said as he held out his hand. Ramina breathed hard and tried to catch her breath before speaking. She couldn't help but smile.

"Thanks, baby," she answered as she slapped hands with her man. They had an unbreakable bond. Although they were lovers, they were best friends.

"I'm hungry," Ramina said as she looked over at him.

"Bitch, me too," Saint playfully said as he displayed his beautiful smile. Then both of them burst out into laughter, and Ramina rolled over and straddled him, playfully hitting him. She leaned down and kissed him after they play fought.

"This really was beautiful. It means the world to me," she said, thinking about their vacation and the thought he put into it. She was on cloud nine.

"And you mean the world to me, pretty girl," Saint answered.

Saint watched as Ramina did her makeup in the mirror across the room. She sat in front of a vanity mirror as she swayed to the music playing in the background. She wore a huge terry cloth robe with a towel wrapped around her head. The smell of sage filled the room, and the smoke danced in the air freely, setting the vibe. Saint sat at the dining table in the middle of the villa. His focus was on the scattered dead men's faces that were on the table. He put the stack of hundred-dollar bills through the money machine and watched as the Benjamin Franklin faces flickered one after another. A loud beep sounded, letting him know that the count was complete. He quickly grabbed the money out of the top of the machine and then wrapped a rubber band around it. He neatly placed the stack in the duffle bag that was near his feet. He always recounted the money to make sure it was right. He wanted to make sure that his purchase money was accurate for his upcoming Cuba trip. Although they were in Aruba that morning, he planned on being in Cuba by the end of the night. Saint had been in the drug game since his teens, but everything changed when he found a heroin connect in Havana, Cuba, while on vacation with Ramina. He had the plug going on seven years, and his empire had skyrocketed since the pipeline was formed. He always scheduled his Cuba trips at the end of a vacation that he and Ramina took. That way, he could avoid the hassle of the US and being under the watchful eyes of the American government. Saint was very strategic, and this was just one of his cautious tactics to remain meticulous.

"So, listen. I'm going to meet you back here in two days. I'm going to shoot this move and be right back," he said as he zipped up the duffle bag.

"OK, babe, I'll be here waiting," Ramina answered as she applied the blush on her cheekbones. She paused and turned around so she could be facing him rather than the mirror. She watched as he walked over to her with his duffle bag in hand. He had a stack of money in his hand and gave it to her.

"This is for some shopping. Zoo is downstairs when you're ready to go. Just call him, and he'll have the car ready for you out front," Saint said, letting her know that he had everything taken care of. Zoo always tagged along with them when they traveled the world.

The car service was waiting outside of the villa to transport him to the private airport. As usual, he chartered a private plane to Cuba so he could meet his connect Alejandro. Ramina took the money and smiled as she examined the stack. She loved the way he spoiled her, and she couldn't wait to hit the shopping district in downtown Aruba. She stood up and jumped into his arms, instantly making him drop his bag. She wrapped her legs around his waist and wrapped her arms around the back of his neck. Saint was just under six feet, so he hovered over her five foot four frame. It was easy for him to scoop her up as he cuffed her plump butt cheeks, feeling her wobbly, soft cheeks.

"My pretty girl," he whispered as he hugged her tightly. She closed her eyes and inhaled the clean, fresh smell of his cologne.

"You're so good to me. Thank you, baby," she said just before she leaned in and kissed him. After their kiss, he let her down to her feet and just stared at her, smiling. She always loved it when he showed his teeth. It was her favorite part of his physical features. The sight alone made her want to have a replay of what they had done earlier that morning.

"You deserve to be treated well. You're perfect. Perfect for me, anyway. You just get a nigga, ya heard me?" Saint said with sincerity.

"You heard me?" Ramina mocked while smiling from ear to ear and playfully making a silly face. She loved mocking his New Orleans accent. His charm melted her, and he didn't even try. It was so effortless with Saint. He always knew how to time things perfectly to make her smile. That Creole-influenced twang got her every time. They both laughed.

"Be safe. I'll be here waiting when you get back," she said as she stood on her tiptoes to give him a peck on the lips. Saint gently smacked her buttocks and squeezed it just before he picked up the duffle bag, heading out the door.

"Forty-eight hours," Saint said as he opened the door to exit.

"Forty-eight hours," Ramina repeated as she stared into the mirror, beginning to apply her mascara. That was something they always said before he went on his Cuba trips. He always made it a brief trip when going to visit his plug.

"Hey," Saint said as he looked back at his woman.

"Yes," she said as she stayed focused on the mirror while tending to her eyelashes.

"Look at me," Saint instructed. He waited until her full focus was on him before he spoke again. Ramina slowly turned toward him and caught him staring at her, smiling widely. His whites and his golds instantly made her smile.

"Yes?" she said beaming.

"I just wanted to look at you again," he said as he stared at her in admiration. After a few seconds of gazing, he quickly left. She sat there, blushing with butterflies in her stomach, staring at the door.

"That's a man right there," she whispered to herself as she shook her head in disbelief at how he could still make her feel like a little girl. His charisma always made Ramina feel a type of way and only solidified that he was the love of her life.

Saint took the elevator to the lobby and checked his watch to see what time it was. Just like he planned, he was in the lobby at nine a.m. sharp. The private resort had some of the best villas in the country, and it was one of Saint's frequent vacationing spots. He walked onto the marble floors that led to the spacious, open lobby where staff moved about the place. The five-star establishment was gorgeous, and the sound of the live Mariachi band serenaded the morning guests. Saint wore an open linen shirt with Armani slacks, Italian cut. As he walked out on the marble floor, he looked over toward the car and saw Zoo sitting there conversing with a beautiful Latina woman. Zoo glanced over and noticed Saint and cut his conversation short to join him.

"Top of the top," Saint smoothly said as he slid a toothpick in his mouth.

"Top of the morning," Zoo responded as he slapped hands with his best friend. They both headed outside of the establishment so they could talk away from the earshot of the other guests and staff.

"How was your night?" Saint said as he gave Zoo a smirk and looked back at the lady who was sitting at the bar.

"Nigga, you see that over there?" Zoo said as he smiled and rubbed his hands together while glancing back as well.

"I see it, for sure," Saint complimented and approved. He shook his head and chuckled at his right-hand man. They had spent the previous day on a yacht together, including the Latina woman, so he was familiar with her. She looked back and saw Saint and Zoo looking at her. She smiled and waved at Saint. Saint slightly smiled and gave her a head nod acknowledging her.

"What?" Zoo asked, knowing Saint wanted to say something. "What? Spill the beans, brody," Zoo said.

"I'm just saying . . . every trip we take, you come with a different girl. Every single time," Saint said.

"Everybody can't be like you and Ramina. See, y'all got something real. All this shit is fake, bro," Zoo explained.

"What you mean exactly?" Saint asked, trying to follow Zoo's thoughts.

"I mean that none of this is real if you really think about it. She wants me because I got the bag and can take her on trips for her to post on social media. And to be honest, I only want her because of that phat ass. Simple math. It's an unspoken transaction that no one likes to talk about," Zoo expertly explained.

"I get it, bruh. I just can't lie down with a bitch I don't have a mental connection with, ya hear me? I mean, I could when I was younger, but now, I'm on some other shit. Catching a nut is only half the pleasure," Saint said.

"I feel that. But until I find someone like that, I'm keeping my options open," said Zoo. He tapped Saint on the chest playfully and looked around like he was about to tell him a secret. "Bro, I let that bitch spit in my mouth." They both burst out into laughter, and Saint shook his head in disbelief.

"Y'all into some freaky shit. What the fuck, man?" Saint asked while laughing.

"You damn right. She loves for me to choke her while I'm hitting it," Zoo explained.

"What?" Saint asked while squinting his eyes.

"This girl is wild as hell, brody. I thought I was about to kill her last night, but she didn't want me to stop. She said she comes harder when she's about to pass out. It's the weirdest shit."

Saint just stayed silent and shook his head as he couldn't wrap his thoughts around the choking thing. He couldn't see how a woman could let a man do that to her. He tried to envision himself choking Ramina but couldn't. In his mind, during sex, a woman should be handled gently and treated like a difficult math problem. This meant slowly taking your time to figure out the intricacies that please her. He knew that sex was about breaking a body's code, not pain. This is why he could make a woman fall in love with him, while others like Zoo couldn't. Before Saint could respond, he saw a black luxury car pull up. He knew that it was for him. He arranged for the car service to pick him up at nine oh five.

"Okay, this me," Saint said as he reached out and slapped hands with Zoo.

"Bet. I'll make sure Ramina is good," Zoo ensured his right-hand man, knowing that would be the next thing Saint would say to him.

"I appreciate you. I'll be right back," Saint confirmed as the car pulled up right in front of him. One of the bellhops went to open the door, and Saint stepped forward to slide in the backseat of the vehicle. The bellhop held his hand up, signaling for Saint to pause. He then looked past him and focused on the group of four men emerging from the elevator, all white men of a certain age. They all looked to be fiftyish. They wore different variations of tropical shirts, and all had deep tans. They were chatting among themselves and had beers in their hand as they approached the car. They also were rolling luggage with their free hands.

"Excuse me, sir," the bellhop said to Saint as he slightly brushed him to the side, clearing the path for the white men approaching. Saint instantly grew offended and frowned at the lack of respect shown for him. Zoo caught wind of Saint's discomfort and immediately went into goon mode and stepped forward.

"Don't get smacked the fuck up out here," Zoo said with his face twisted up in anger.

As always, Saint remained calm and gently tapped Zoo's back and whispered, "It's all good. Stand down." He didn't want Zoo to go berserk. He knew his friend well enough to know that he had no problem with turning the small situation into a chaotic scene. Zoo took a deep breath and stepped back as Saint requested.

"Sir, I apologize, but this service is for Mr. Regis," the valet said as he didn't even take the time to look at Zoo. As the men approached, they dropped their luggage and like ants to sugar, the bellboys hustled to pick up their bags.

Who is this guy? Saint thought to himself, offended. He stepped back and closely watched as everyone seemed to want to cater to the group of men. He watched as the men all slid into the back of the spacious car, and the man with the open shirt and bone-white hair was the last to enter the vehicle. The man had a head full of white hair and a neatly trimmed goatee. His teeth were pearly white. He reached into his pocket and pulled out a diamond-encrusted money clip as he watched the last of the bags being loaded into the trunk. He then peeled off Benjamin Franklins and tipped each bellboy that was in his sight. By the way that everyone was so attentive to him, one could tell the respect level that everyone had for the man. Saint and Zoo watched as the man got inside the car and slowly cruised out of the resort's lot.

"Our money spends like his," Zoo said as he reached into his pocket and pulled out a rubber-banded knot of one-hundred-dollar bills and fifties. He waved it in their faces as he had a smug look on his face.

"Put that away," Saint said calmly and in a low tone. He then leaned over to a young valet worker and asked him the question that was on his mind.

"Who was that?" Saint questioned.

"That's Regis Epstein," he answered while leaning in and keeping his voice low. He then continued to fill in Saint. "He owns this entire resort. He actually has a few of them here and also in the United States. Big spender . . . big tipper. Everyone wants to get in his good graces to catch him on one of his generous nights. He's a fucking billionaire," the man said with excitement.

"Gotcha," Saint said while nodding, taking in the information. He then realized that it wasn't all about money. Sometimes, power.

Saint reached into his pocket and slipped the valet a hundred-dollar bill for the insight. The valet's eyes lit up, and he quickly thanked him while sliding the money into his pocket. The valet looked beyond Saint and waved over a second car to pull up. Saint followed his eyes and saw the car. He slapped hands with Zoo and watched as the valet opened the door for him.

"In a minute, beloved," Saint said to Zoo just before he smoothly slid into the backseat of the car with a duffle bag in hand. He was on his way to get on a jet to order one hundred kilos of the purest heroin in the world.

Chapter Five

Iron Eagle

Saint stood at the desk, looking in the eyes of the blond, blue-eyed receptionist. He was slightly agitated as he rested his hands on the counter, waiting for a response from the lady that stood behind the desk. He stared at her as she typed into her computer.

"I'm sorry, Mr. Cole. We don't have any charters available until tomorrow evening," she said as she shook her head as she scanned her log list, running her finger down the screen. Moments before, she had informed him that one of the pilots had called in ill, and his scheduled Cuba flight wasn't available. This presented a problem for Saint because Alejandro was very finicky about promptness. He knew it was a flight that he could not miss.

"I scheduled a flight a month ahead of time. There has to be something you could do," Saint said in a low, calm tone, thinking about the potential hiccup in business that this missed flight might cause.

"I'm sorry, sir. My hands are tied. I can check to see if there are any outgoing commercial flights. The airport is just down the street," she suggested, trying to accommodate their mishap. Saint instantly knew that was not a possibility because of the security and customs process that commercial flights entailed. He could not chance being caught with that amount of money. It would cause a red flag for sure. Although he didn't transport the dope back, he did indeed directly bring the cash to the plug Alejandro and set up the deal. This was a shopping process that had to be done by him personally, or else it just wouldn't happen.

"That's not an option. I fly private, ma'am," Saint said as he turned around and looked on the runway. He saw a large Gulfstream G6 sitting on the runway with the steps let down. It was the grandfather of the fleet and one of the biggest jets money could buy. Saint noticed it immediately because he had been eyeing it for some time now. His money was only long enough to charter the smaller ones, but he promised himself he would charter a bigger jet one day. "What about that? Is that jet available?"

"Sorry, that jet is reserved for . . ." the receptionist said but paused when another man approached the desk. Saint followed her eyes and noticed that it was the same man from the resort. It was the white-haired man that Saint had seen earlier. Saint watched as the group of men that he was with earlier filed out of the private lounge with a few younger women around them. Obviously, they were having a good time. The drinks in their hands and laughter were evidence of it. They all headed out the door and toward the awaiting jet. Regis stopped at the desk after overhearing the problem involving Saint.

"Hi, Jan," the guy said with a big smile on his face.

"Oh, hello, Mr. Epstein," Jan said enthusiastically.

"Hey. I didn't mean any harm earlier at the resort. We were kind of in a rush, and the staff knew that," Regis said with sincerity.

"No worries," Saint replied.

"I'm Regis," the man said as he extended his hand.

"I'm S—" Saint began, but Regis cut him off midsentence.

"Saint Cole," Regis said, finishing his words for him.

"Yeah, how did you know?" Saint said as he squinted and shook his hand.

"You're going to Cuba, right?" Regis asked.

"Yea . . ." Saint said, confused, not knowing how Regis knew so much about him.

"Jan, he can ride with us," Regis said as he looked over at the receptionist and winked. "Well, that's if you *want* to. We are heading over there for the weekend anyway."

"Sure . . ." Saint said skeptically. However, he wasn't about to turn it down because he needed to get there.

"Walk with me. Let's talk," Regis said as he motioned Saint to follow him outside onto the runway. Saint picked up his bag and followed him out. As they exited the building, they stood on the runway and talked.

"You're going to see Alejandro, right?" Regis said nonchalantly as he slid his hands in his shorts and casually walked.

"Maybe . . ." Saint answered, not wanting to expose his hand to the stranger. His mind started to churn, wondering how Regis knew so much.

"You don't have to worry. Alejandro is an old friend of mine. You see that logo," Regis said as he pointed at the jet with the Eagle on it. It was a logo of an eagle that read *RE Enterprises* across the bottom. "That's my logo. I own this fleet," Regis informed him.

"So, this is yours?" Saint asked as he waved at the private charter building.

"Yes, sir," Regis answered.

"Alejandro recommended that you use my company to handle your business, correct?"

"Yeah, that's right," Saint confirmed, as the picture started to look clearer to him. Saint remembered that Alejandro suggested that he fly from Aruba to Cuba and, shortly after, suggested RE Enterprise as an airline. Saint then understood that Regis's private airline was a pipeline for Alejandro's heroin business. It all made sense. That immediately made Saint more comfortable with Regis.

They were both in the same business. Saint remembered that the valet mentioned that he owned the resort, and now Saint was learning that he owned the private jet company as well. *Oh, he papered up for real,* Saint thought to himself as he did the math in his head.

"You're not the only person that comes through here that Alejandro deals with," Regis explained. "You can ride with us. We will get you there. Come on," Regis said as he patted Saint on the back. They headed toward the jet, and while walking, Regis pulled out a big Cuban cigar and lit it. He puffed it slowly and held his head back, blowing smoke circles in the sky. Saint observed closely and watched the older man who seemed not to have a care in the world. The closer they got to the jet, the louder the sound of the jet propellers got.

Saint climbed the stairs and entered the cabin of the jet. He was greeted by a gorgeous redheaded woman who looked more like a supermodel than a stewardess. Her big double D breasts and long legs looked like she had stepped right off a fashion runway and then came to her job as a flight attendant. Her full lips made her look plastic. She resembled a real-life Barbie doll.

"Hello, Mr. Epstein. Welcome aboard," she said as she held a glass plate in front of her. It had three rows of a white powdery substance on it. Also, a rolled-up dollar bill next to it moved slightly around on the glass. She raised the plate so that it was chest level with Mr. Epstein.

He wasted no time as he smiled and picked up the dollar bill, putting it into his nostrils. He made a loud snorting noise, sniffing a line and swiftly tossing his head back to avoid drainage. Regis smiled and whispered, "Thanks, babe." Then he walked into the cabin, and Saint was right behind him. As Saint stepped up, the stewardess offered the plate to him, but he put up his hand, rejecting the offer. Saint didn't do drugs, and he wasn't about to start.

He was blown away by the upscale interior design. He had been on jets before, but this one was different. The pristine architecture was simply breathtaking. The smell of flowers invaded Saint's senses as a plethora of beautiful, colorful bouquets were placed throughout the joint. The plane was equipped with marble floors, neon lights, and had a full bar accompanied by a bartender. It resembled a classy lounge more so than an aircraft. Saint looked around in awe as he observed his surroundings. He thought that he was getting money, but after seeing Regis's private jet, he understood that there were levels to it. Regis introduced Saint to each of his three friends as they moved about the cabin. Saint greeted them all, and they welcomed him with open arms. Regis and Saint ended up at the bar as they both grabbed a seat on the stools.

"Do you drink scotch?" Regis asked while he grinned, displaying his white porcelain teeth.

"Sure," Saint answered as he got comfortable on the stool. Regis immediately turned toward the bartender and put up two fingers.

"Coming right up, Mr. Epstein," the Latino bartender said as he snatched two Cognac glasses off of the back display and poured the drinks. Just as Regis turned back to talk to Saint, the pilot's voice sounded through the jet's speakers.

"Hello, Mr. Epstein and guests. We are about to take off, headed to Cuba. The flight is just under three hours, so sit back and enjoy, everyone," he said just before logging off.

Saint felt the power of the jet take off, and he became slightly tense. All the others on the flight were enjoying themselves, laughing while doing blow. Regis saw Saint's uneasiness and raised his glass and waved it, signaling for a toast. Saint picked up his glass and obliged Regis.

They tapped glasses, making a chiming noise that sounded throughout the jet. They then downed the drinks, and a conversation between them ensued.

"So, tell me about yourself. What are you into besides your business with my guy, Alejandro?" Regis questioned.

"This is all I know. My business with Alejandro is my only business," Saint answered honestly. He was a stone-cold hustler. That was all he was about.

"What a shame . . ." Regis said under his breath as he shook his head and downed the last swallow of his drink.

"Come again?" Saint said, feeling as if he were being belittled.

"It's . . . just . . . Can I be honest with you?" Regis asked.

"Absolutely," Saint said, looking Regis directly in the eye, trying to find out his angle, but also giving him a stern look to let him know that disrespect would not be tolerated. Regis returned the stare, but his eyes weren't ones of malice. He seemed to be sincere in his concern and tone.

"I hate to see your people get caught in the trap," he stated as he waved his hands while speaking.

"Your people? Trap?" Saint questioned, slightly offended.

"Yes. The trap of generational curses."

"Hmm," Saint said, listening carefully, wanting to hear more of what he was saying.

"Obviously, you're a bright guy. You've made it to this level of the field you're in. However, where is the maturation? Where is the growth? I mean . . . the United States was built on dirty money, so I'm not knocking what you do. Sometimes, to build a firm foundation, you have to play on the devil's playground."

"You damn right," Saint said, agreeing with what the older white man was discoursing.

"I want you to listen closely to what I'm about to say . . ." Regis requested. Saint nodded his head to affirm that he was all ears. Regis paused and looked Saint directly in the eyes and stated, "The first blocks of your foundation . . . should be the only ones that should have to touch the dirt."

"Well said," Saint replied. He understood where Regis was coming from, and he realized that he was right.

"The issue with your people . . . no disrespect . . . but the issue is the unwillingness to go legit. If you're into a shady business, there is no way your kids should be too. Does this make sense? At some point, you have to have an exit strategy and turn the dirty money clean," Regis answered straightforwardly.

Saint listened carefully and thought deep and hard about what Regis had said. He didn't know if it was the drugs or booze that had Regis so open to talk with him. Nevertheless, Saint was smart enough to comprehend that insight was better than money, and it wasn't every day that he got a chance to sit and talk with billionaires. Saint soaked up the game received from Regis, and they had an intimate conversation for the entire duration of the flight. Saint had gained an ally on that trip, and he understood the power in that. Before exiting, they traded numbers, and Regis invited Saint to his home after his business with Alejandro. Saint gladly accepted.

Chapter Six

Birds and the Keys

Havana, Cuba, was hot and dry as the sun beamed down. The tourist and airport workers moved around outside of the terminal. Cuba had no frills or fancy architectural structures. Their technology and landscapes were at least fifteen years behind the United States. It was cut and dry. They had one facility for incoming jets and planes for the entire region. There wasn't any classism in the country because almost everyone was poor and living beneath their means. Only the government or those who were connected to it were well off. That and the Cuban Cartel. It was cartel land that Saint was in, but he didn't worry because he knew the leader of it personally.

The people there were kind and humble. Having nothing usually made people appreciate life and others a tad bit more. That's one of the reasons why Saint loved the country. It always humbled him. It was in the afternoon, and local kids were scattered around, peddling Cuban-themed T-shirts and paintings to the incoming tourists. It seemed as if every product had faces of mostly Fidel Castro or "Che" Guevara printed on it. Ever since Obama had mended the United States' tumultuous relationship with the country, it became more of a tourist destination.

A little brown boy ran up to Saint and pulled at his shirt, causing him to look down.

"Dos," he said as he held up two fingers. He waved the Cuban bandanna around. Saint smiled at the kid and respected his hustle.

"Dos?" Saint repeated as he held up two fingers as well. The young boy smiled, showing his brown teeth. The boy had a black eye and fat lip, which made Saint feel sorry for him.

"*Sí*," the young boy said while nodding his head up and down.

"Bet. I got you, li'l man," Saint responded as he returned the smile and reached into his pocket. The young boy's eyes lit up when he saw Saint's gold teeth. He jumped up and down in joy and pointed to them as if they were majestic. In their country, seeing something like that was like seeing a unicorn.

"Oh, you're talking about my teeth?" Saint asked while smiling even bigger. "You like that gold, huh, li'l man?" Saint ran his finger across his bottom row to signal what he was saying to the boy.

Saint reached into the top of his T-shirt and pulled out a small gold chain that he had tucked away inside. It had a small charm hanging from it. It was a solid gold baby saint with Black boy features. On the back, his initials were engraved. It read *SVC*.

Saint reached around his neck to unclasp it. He smoothly unhooked it and placed it on his new little friend's neck. Saint let the charm fall to li'l man's chest, and he stepped back to check him out.

"Now, you a fly young nigga," Saint smoothly said as he crossed his hands and stood in the classic hustler's pose. The little boy was so happy and joyous as he mimicked Saint.

The child slapped hands with Saint and looked down at the gold around his neck. He teared up because he was so happy. He didn't even own a pair of shoes, so a chain was everything to him. He quickly wiped the tears away, but he never stopped smiling.

"*Gracias. Gracias,*" the young boy said, meaning thank you in Spanish.

"*De nada,*" Saint responded, meaning you're welcome. Saint didn't know a lot of Spanish, but he knew the bare minimum to get by. Saint then pulled out some pesos and slid a bill to him. The young boy, in return, handed him the Cuban bandanna.

"Yeah, this some fly shit, ya hear me?" Saint asked as he folded it up and tied it around his head. Saint put his hand on his chest and said, "*Me llamo,* Saint," introducing himself.

"*Me llamo,* Luca," the young boy said as he tapped his chest and smiled widely.

"Bet. My nigga, Luca," Saint said as he slapped hands with him. The young boy nodded his head in appreciation and walked off with his chest poking out, excited about his new chain. A group of his friends crowded around him and examined the chain in awe. Saint watched as the boys slapped fives with him and made him feel like a king.

People of different ethnicities stood on the curb, waiting for their turn to hop in a taxi. Saint stood on the curb as well and heard distant voices approaching him. He looked back and saw Regis and his party. Saint had opted to exit the jet as soon as it landed. At that time, they weren't done partying, so he excused himself, knowing he had to meet his plug. A black SUV pulled up to the curb. It stuck out because it was the only vehicle that was remotely modern on the entire street. Saint watched as they hopped in and cruised away. They were all so high that they didn't even acknowledge Saint as they brushed past him to get in the truck.

Saint recalled their conversation on the flight and realized that Regis had given him a lot to think about. During their brief encounter, they talked about everything from politics to sports, but mainly business. Saint learned that each one of his friends on that flight was a billionaire. Other than Regis, a senator, an oil tycoon, and an NFL team owner were on that jet. Saint watched them party like rock stars with the young women for the entire flight. One wouldn't know that they were such prominent figures by how wild they were. A single leaked photo from that jet ride could have ruined all of their lives. He saw someone waving from afar as he looked up the street. It was a short Cuban man with a straw fedora. He instantly recognized him. It was his usual driver, Pedro, waving him over to the car. Saint walked over to the vehicle, and the man opened the door for him.

"Mi amigo, Saint," the short man said in excitement as he displayed his snaggletoothed smile.

"Peace, beloved. Good to see you," Saint said as he placed his hand on Pedro's shoulder and gave it a slight squeeze. The humble man bowed his head and smiled, genuinely happy to see him. What he got paid to transport Saint on that one day took care of his family for three months. In his eyes, Saint was a pure blessing from God. Saint ducked his head, slid in, and got comfortable. He knew they had a long ride ahead. He was on his way deep into the jungle, where not many people went. The entire town knew whose territory that belonged to, and it wasn't to be tested. It was time to visit the plug, Alejandro.

Beautiful green leaves and vibrant flowers grew everywhere. Rich, dark soil covered the ground, and hundreds of chirping sounds blended together to make a unique, cohesive ambiance. It was nearing dusk, and the sun was falling for the day. The temperature had cooled off, and the air had tons of moisture in it. Saint took a deep breath and closed his eyes as he felt a sense of relaxation. He bopped up and down while on the back of a brown thoroughbred horse as they made their way through the jungle. His small duffle bag was by his crotch, tucked securely as they made their way through the wilderness.

His male guide led the way on a horse as well. The guide was shirtless and shoeless and looked to be in his early teens. He held a long stick in his hand as he rode, using it as a lead stick to push away the low-hanging branches and clear the path for Saint and him. As always, the guide never said one word to Saint. He just met him at the pickup location where the road ended and then took him to his boss, Alejandro. Saint's driver would always park and wait for his return, no matter how long it took.

At first, the long jungle journey used to make Saint uneasy. However, after a few trips, he started appreciating the nature trot. The smell of the damp earth combined with old, fallen leaves was unique. The earthy smell had an automatic calming effect on a human, and Saint experienced it every time. He would always look straight up through the tall trees that hovered over them to see if he could catch a glimpse of exotic birds that he probably wouldn't see anywhere else. The jungle never disappointed him. The colorful creatures would dip in and out of sight, flying from branch to branch. The small crevices through the tall treetops allowed the sky's light to illuminate the area. He knew that they only had a little while longer before it would be completely dark, and this is why arriving on time was so important when going to see Alejandro.

Saint wiped his brow as the sweat dripped off his forehead. He felt the bandanna that Luca had given him was still tied around his head. He had almost forgotten that he had it on. As Saint looked ahead, he saw the big castle sitting on a hill. The sky opened up. They had finally cleared the jungle. Two gun towers that resembled lighthouses stood on opposite sides of each other. Both stood fifty feet vertically. The towers were made of a beautiful gray stone wall, and a large light sat at the top of it for night vision. One sat on each side of the home overlooking the entire property. One gunman was in each tower, both armed with scoped high-powered rifles. The level of protection never ceased to amaze Saint every time that he visited. Unlike back in the States, the police feared the gangsters—not the other way around, and Saint could respect that, being a Black man in America. He admired the tenacity of the drug lords to rebel against the authorities. The willingness to go to war with the police was the main thing that kept the peace. The mere thought that the other side would push that button made the police think twice about friction. Sometimes, that's all you need for peace . . . the fear of knowing that the other side *would* push the button.

They made it to the entrance, which was protected by a tall steel gate that wrapped around the entire compound. Barbed wires were at the top of the gates, and it looked more like a luxury prison rather than a home. The guide gave a hand signal to the guard, and moments later, the harsh noise of the steel moving sounded, and the gates parted open. Saint hopped off of the horse and grabbed his bag. He then walked across the land and entered the private property. As Saint made his way to the front door, he saw Alejandro's wife waiting for him. She stood there, smiling with her hands on her hips. She waved him in, and Saint smiled at her.

"Hello, Magalia," Saint said as he smiled and leaned in to kiss her cheek.

"Hello, Saint. So good to see you," she said, speaking perfect English. She was in her midforties and was a beautiful, middle-aged woman. She was about ten years younger than her husband, Alejandro. She was full-blooded Cuban, and her olive skin glowed like none other. Her dark hair was neatly pulled back, and her smile was welcoming and warming as usual. She had a big beautiful smile that warmed Saint every time he saw her. She had a single silver tooth in the far left side of her mouth, and it was like her signature. Saint always remembered that shiny cap every time she opened her mouth.

"Alejandro is in the back with the kids," she said as she stepped into the house and made her way into the back. Saint followed her as they started walking down the long foyer.

The inside was amazing to the eye. Every time Saint visited their home, he was blown away by the stunning Gothic, old-fashioned design. It almost made him feel like he was underground. The rocky ceilings and gray stonewall gave it a vintage theme. The long corridor was just ahead of him, which led to Alejandro's main living quarters. The hall resembled a high-end cave. Wooden lanterns were lined on the walls to provide lighting, and the smell of cedar was prominent.

As they made their way to the end of the hall, a large, sliding barnyard door stood there. Magalia reached for the door and slid it open, revealing their beautiful, modern home. The open floor plan gave it a grand appearance. One wouldn't even think that they were in Cuba by looking at it. It looked more like a high-end condominium in the middle of Manhattan.

The color scheme had shifted from what it was when you first entered. The white marble floors and light walls brightened up the setting. An AK-47 rifle was on the floor, propped up against the wall as if it were an umbrella. It was just casually there. Saint learned that Alejandro kept assault rifles all through the house as if they were a part of the décor. His family was so used to having guns around that they paid it no mind. It tripped Saint out every time he came over to see the ins and outs of cartel life.

Saint stepped in and saw Alejandro wrestling with his two young brown boys on the floor. They were laughing and horse playing as they reenacted a big-time wrestling match.

"Alejandro, Saint has arrived," Magalia said with enthusiasm as she stepped to the side so that he could get a clear view of their guest. She walked over to the kitchen area, put on an apron, and checked the food that she was preparing. The smell of Cuban cuisine filled the air, and Saint instantly remembered how good of a cook Magalia was.

"Aye, Saint, Amigo," Alejandro yelled with genuine excitement as he stood up from the ground and threw his hands in the air. Saint instantly smiled, feeling the love from his dope connect. Every time he came to Cuba, they made him feel like family, and it was much appreciated.

Alejandro walked toward Saint with his arms open, welcoming a hug. He wore a black silk shirt and well-tailored Italian cut slacks. Versace slippers were on his feet, and his whole style was player. He had brown skin and looked like an African American. The only thing that suggested his Cuban heritage was his soft, curly hair. He wore a five o'clock shadow for a beard and was slim built.

Look at this smooth old nigga, Saint thought to himself as he approached and hugged him tightly. After their embrace, Alejandro cupped Saint's face and smiled, looking at him directly in the eyes.

"You look so much like my brother. It gets me every time," Alejandro said while shaking his head in disbelief and smirking at the same time. Although Saint was of no kin to him, he reminded him of his deceased brother so much. Saint was like a younger version of him, and it always blew his mind. That was one of the reasons he took a liking to Saint years back while meeting him at a local restaurant.

"You always say that," Saint responded, knowing that Alejandro always enjoyed seeing him. Saint didn't mind one bit. He found a plug of a lifetime in Alejandro, so he wasn't complaining at all. They had built a strong bond over the years, and Alejandro gave Saint whatever he wanted, as far as heroin was concerned. Alejandro owned over 500 acres of land in Cuba. He grew many things like tobacco, hemp, and his number one breadwinner . . . opium poppy plants.

Opium poppies were flowers from which heroin was made after an eight-step process. It was by far the most addictive drug in the world, and no one produced more in the world than Alejandro. His lavish home reflected his vast wealth and success as a leader of his Cuban drug cartel.

"What's good, fellas?" Saint asked, as he looked past Alejandro and saw the two young boys, both 9 years old. They were twins and Alejandro's only namesakes.

"Hey, Saint," one of the boys yelled in excitement.

"What's up, Saint?" the other boy yelled right after. Alejandro raised his children speaking English, knowing that it would be an essential skill to have. He always planned on sending his boys to college in the US, not wanting them to follow his footsteps in the drug trade. However, in the meantime, he did not hide or shelter them from what he did. He wanted them to know both sides of the game, just in case the US thing didn't pan out. Saint handed a small bag over to Alejandro. He peeked in the bag and smiled at Saint.

"You come bearing gifts," Alejandro said while smiling. He tossed it over to his son, who caught it excitedly.

"Count it up, boys," Alejandro instructed his boys. They eagerly hopped up and started dancing, loving to get a chance to play with the money machine. The boys raced to the kitchen table and dumped the money on it. One of the boys ran to grab the money counter from a closet, and shortly after, they were beginning the counting process. Alejandro looked over at his wife as she stirred the pot of shrimp in coconut sauce. She always made sure she cooked a good old-fashioned Cuban meal when Saint came around.

"How long until the meal, Mama?" Alejandro asked his lady as he looked at her with admiration. She smiled as she looked up to answer her husband of over fifteen years.

"About an hour, papi," she answered as she wiped her hands on her apron.

"Great! We have time for a cigar," Alejandro said as he winked at Saint and headed toward the door that led to his basement.

Saint followed Alejandro down the stairs. The tavern-style staircase was made of cherry oak, which led to Alejandro's man cave. It looked like an old-school cigar lounge, equipped with a pool table and an old-school jukebox. A walk-in cigar humidor was surrounded by glass. They made their way over to the humidor and stepped in to handpick themselves a Cuban cigar.

"Heard you had an eventful trip here," Alejandro said as he picked up a cigar and slid it under his nose, appreciating the homegrown optimum stick.

"Word got back to you quick," Saint responded as he picked up a cigar of his own.

"Of course. I know everything that's going on in my territory," Alejandro confirmed. They casually walked around the humidor, which had rows and rows of hand-rolled cigars and looked through the selection.

"Yo, what's the story with that guy?" Saint asked.

"Who? Regis?" Alejandro asked.

"Yeah," said Saint.

"A rich asshole," Alejandro said, sending them both into a small chuckle. He then continued. "He's a necessary evil that I use for my business. He makes it possible for me to transport my product throughout the world with ease with his private fleet. But to be honest, I don't care for him too much," he admitted.

"Oh, yeah?" Saint said, trying to understand who Regis was.

"Yeah, he has a dark side that I don't agree with," Alejandro said as he exited the room and headed over to the lounge chairs.

Saint thought that Regis was an excellent plug to have and wondered why Alejandro was down talking him.

There has to be more to the story, Saint thought as he followed him out and joined him for a smoke. Saint didn't ask any further about Regis, but he definitely was curious about his new acquaintance. The financial game that Regis had laid on him during the flight had Saint's mind open to expansion and leaving the drug game. Regis's words really stuck with Saint, and the thought of having an exit plan didn't seem like a bad idea. Saint thought that maybe Alejandro didn't like the thought of Regis taking one of his drug distributors away. Little did Saint know, however, that Alejandro was trying to protect him from the devils that hid underneath the surface . . .

Chapter Seven

Cougars

"Okay, get ready for bed, guys. Tell Saint good night," Magalia said as she cleared the table, collecting the plates off of it.

She, Alejandro, and the kids had just had dinner with Saint, compliments of Magalia's excellent cooking. While eating, they talked and laughed together about life. Not once did they speak about drugs because what was understood never needed to be explained.

Once Saint left with the bricks, he would see Pandora, and then he would leave them with Pedro. That was the routine, and by the time he returned home to New Orleans, a pallet of heroin bricks would be waiting for him by way of hidden compartments inside of a U-Haul truck. Saint never asked about the intricacies of the operation as far as the transportation of the drug. Alejandro had a well-oiled machine, and his reach was substantial. All of the people in Cuba worked together as a unit. Cuba treated drugs differently than people in the States. Drugs weren't as taboo and were almost looked at as a religion. It was their country's primary source of money, and it had its own intricate network.

Saint stuck out his hand to give the boys a pound as they excused themselves from the table.

"Holla at y'all next time," Saint said as he playfully rubbed their heads, messing up their hair.

"See ya later, Saint," one said.

"Bye, Saint," the other boy said as they both hugged their father and ran upstairs out of sight. Magalia put the dishes in the sink and then walked over to Saint.

"I'm about to get the boys ready for bed. It was good seeing you, Saint," Magalia said as she bent down to kiss him on the cheek and hugged him.

"Thank you so much for dinner, and it was good seeing you too," Saint replied as he grinned.

"You're stopping by to see my sister before you leave, right?" Magalia asked.

"Absolutely. I'm going by in the morning before I leave," Saint confirmed.

"Okay, I'll let her know to expect you," Magalia said.

"Thank you so much," Saint replied.

"You know she has a thing for you, right?" Alejandro playfully asked while smiling.

"She does not," Magalia said as she playfully hit her husband.

"She wants to be his cougar," Alejandro said before bursting out in laughter.

"Oh, hush. She just likes him. He reminds her of Bo when he was younger," Magalia said as she mentioned Alejandro's deceased brother. Alejandro and his brother had met them both at the same time, decades ago, during a double date. That was how their blended families began many moons ago.

Saint remained silent, smiled, and shook his head. Magalia gave her husband a quick peck on the lips and headed toward the stairs.

"Take care, Saint," she yelled before she disappeared up the stairs.

"You too," Saint yelled to her before focusing on his plug. Alejandro reached under the table and grabbed the duffle bag. The bag was filled with some of the most potent dope in the world. Saint could step on it multiple times and still have the best dope in the country; it was that strong and pure.

"All jokes aside, make sure you go see Pandora before you leave. It's an important step to complete the process. The one time I didn't ask for the spiritual protection . . . I lost my brother."

"Sorry to hear that," Saint said. That had been the first time Alejandro ever went into detail about his brother's death.

"It's okay, my amigo. Just make sure to remember, whatever you do, right or wrong . . . take prayers with you," Alejandro said, with genuineness in his eyes. He said it, knowing that Saint needed to hear that wisdom. He had a gut feeling that Saint was preparing to get into things that he had no idea about. Saint's chance meeting with Regis made him uneasy. If it were anyone else, Alejandro wouldn't have given two shits about it, but he saw his brother in Saint and wanted to forewarn him without coming outright and saying what was on his mind.

Saint lay in bed in his hotel, and the sounds of the simple, old-fashioned alarm clock rang. It was 9:04 exactly. It was the morning after, and he would leave Cuba in a few hours. He just needed to make one stop before he left the country. He looked over and saw his duffle bag right next to the bed, and he always got a rush when copping drugs there. He knew that he would multiply those squares, put his stamp on them, and flood the bayou in a week.

He got up and took a hot shower, letting the water cascade down his body. The hot water helped wake him up, and after a few minutes, he stepped out and wrapped himself in a towel. He stood in front of the mirror and heard his phone buzz. He looked down at the screen and saw that it was a text from Regis.

Let's have a drink this evening. Talk business . . .

Saint picked up his phone to reply.

I would love to. But flight chartered to leave in a few hours.

Saint put his phone down after pushing the *send* button. He applied shaving cream on his head to prepare for a shave. To his surprise, Regis shot a text back immediately.

Charter was changed to tomorrow night and upgraded to the G5.

Saint nodded his head, remembering the plushness of the luxury aircraft.

Bet.

Saint put down his phone and continued to shave. He instructed Pedro to meet him in the lobby at nine thirty sharp. He sped up the process of shaving, and as he ran the razor across his head, he jumped in pain.

"Fuck!" he said under his breath as he turned his head and looked in the mirror to see the damage. He noticed that he had scraped his head and caused blood to trickle from it. He quickly grabbed a piece of tissue and applied pressure to it to stop the bleeding. He took care of the scratch and got dressed, grabbed the bricks, and headed over to Pandora's district to see her.

Saint had arrived in the Santeria district where Pandora's home was located. His driver, Pedro, had parked the car at the end of the block as he always did, not wanting to drive on the block and interrupt the festivities. The sight of children playing in the streets always made Saint get a feeling of nostalgia from back when he was younger. Those were the only times, while in Cuba, when Saint was reminded of home. The look wasn't similar, but the feeling was. A child's joy was a universal language. That particular district was one known for Santeria rituals, so the sounds of music, drums, and singing were always prevalent there. It was lively. In some ways, it also mirrored summertime on Bourbon Street, just grimier and less glamorous.

Heavy doses of graffiti were drawn on the abandoned buildings and sides of houses. The symbols and drawings were ones of various crosses, abstract art, voodoo dolls, and skeleton heads. To some not familiar with the practice, it might seem scary, but most often, people fear what they don't truly understand. The uninformed would call it voodoo and think of it as spooky or satanic. However, it wasn't evil at all. Europeans gave this religion a negative jacket, but that's only because they didn't understand it. It wasn't for them. It was for the "chosen ones," people of color. The religion of Santeria was merely living descendants connecting with deceased ancestors, asking for help while also praising them.

Saint casually walked down the street, easily blending in with the locals. He carried his duffle bag full of bricks in one hand and slightly held the other arm out. He did so to balance himself while toting the heavy baggage. Kids were running around, laughing, and having a good time, as usual. He approached Pandora's spot, and, like always, the entry was wide open . . . open to whoever wanted to come and get prayer or guidance from her. Pandora was known to be a well respected *oshun*.

An oshun is a spirit, a deity, or a goddess that reflects one of the manifestations of God in the Ifá and Yoruba religions that are practiced heavily in Cuba. Pandora opened her home for all of the community to come. They held her up and protected her faithfully. She was a treasure to the people. Oshun is the deity of the river and fresh water, luxury, pleasure, sexuality, and fertility. She is known to be connected to destiny and foresight. This is why Saint needed to see her. She was his spiritual shield and an insurance policy for the wolves of the game. He had the upper hand on all traffickers in the States just because of this one lone factor. Pandora was his secret weapon.

As Saint crossed the threshold of the door, he noticed that salt was sprinkled on the floor of the steps. Pandora once told Saint that salt helped keep evil spirits away, and that was the reason she did it faithfully. The crunching noise of his shoe against the salt sounded with each step taken.

He proceeded to walk up the narrow staircase, and when he got to the top, he noticed a broom was standing upside down while leaning against the wall. That served a very important purpose that Saint would eventually find out about.

He walked into the home, and instantly, the smell of burning sage invaded his senses. The distinct scent was strong, and clouds danced in the air, making it nearly impossible to see clearly. It resembled fog on a cold Sunday morning. Saint walked in, and the smoke made it seem as if he were in a dream. The smell of the sage relaxed him as he made his way toward the back where Pandora usually was. Although he had no number or direct line to her, she always seemed to be expecting him whenever he arrived. As Saint walked through the hanging beads that separated the rooms, as always, Pandora was in the back corner at a table waiting patiently.

The process that was about to occur was called "baptizing the bricks," and after urging from Alexandro, it was a step that he never missed. With Pandora's blessing, he had the utmost confidence that moving the batch of drugs wouldn't cause him any strife or heartache to himself or his team back home.

"Saint, I've been expecting you," Pandora said while waving him over to her as he smiled.

The room was dim because it had no windows. Only the flickering candles provided the lighting. As Saint walked deeper into the room, he noticed that it was much cooler than the rest of the house. It sent chills up his spine, but not because he was fearful. The sudden climate change caused his body to react in that way.

"Hey, Pandora. How are you?" Saint asked as he approached the table. Saint always thought Pandora was one of the most beautiful older women that he had ever seen. He always was enamored by her gorgeousness every time he was in her presence. Her head wrap was multicolored, and it kept her hair hidden . . . all accept the single gray locs that hung freely to the left of her forehead.

"I'm doing just fine. How are you doing, handsome?" she said as she stared at him with a warm smile. "Have a seat," she instructed as she waved at the chair in front of her table. Saint did as he was told and took a seat while setting the bag of dope at his feet.

"I'm good. Thanks for asking," Saint answered with his boyish charm.

"Before we start, do you want to ask your ancestors anything? Anything troubling you or you need help with?" she asked.

"Nothing more than what's in this bag. I'll save those requests for if I ever really need it," Saint answered.

"Smart man," Pandora said as she smiled and tapped her temple with her index finger. She moved the crystals around that were scattered all over the table, and Saint dug into the duffle bag. He glanced at the wall behind Pandora and noticed a Medusa head, hand-drawn on the wall. He was a big fan of Greek mythology and instantly recognized the woman's character with a head full of snakes and beautiful eyes. He had never before seen that painting while visiting Pandora. Maybe it was a new drawing that was recently added.

"Medusa . . ." he whispered as he stared at the painting. Pandora followed his eyes and looked at the drawing as well.

"No, baby. That's not Medusa. That's a painting of my great-great-great-grandmother. See, you Americans believe anything them white people tell you. Not us . . . We know the truth. That image has been made famous by white-washed tales and Greek mythology. But the truth is . . . Those are not snakes that you see on her head. Those are long locs like the ones on mines," she said as she grabbed one of the gray locs that was hanging in her face. "And her skin wasn't pale. It was dark and brown like yours and mine. Her beauty was so captivating, they switched the truth and sold it to y'all in story form. They steal everything from us and sell it."

"Are you serious?" Saint asked as his mind started to think deeper.

"Yes, I'm afraid I am. That stone that you turn into if you look at her . . . well, that's partially true," Pandora said as she looked down at Saint's crotch area and smiled. Pandora then went back to moving her crystals around. Saint smiled as his mind was blown by the new information that he had just received. He always learned something new when he visited Pandora.

As he placed the bricks on the table, he noticed that she was staring at him. It took him by surprise because she had never looked at him before the way she was looking at him on this day. She had a smirk on her face and didn't flinch or look away when he caught her staring. Pandora was too grown to hide her intentions. She was straightforward and unwavering.

He went back to placing the bricks on the table, thinking that he was tripping. As he set another brick of dope on the table, he heard her voice whisper his name.

"Saint," she said softly as she moved her hand onto his. His eyes instantly shot to her hand and then up to her lustful eyes. "You look just like him," she continued.

"Huh?" he said, pretending as if he didn't know what she was talking about, but he did.

"I'm going to give it to you today," Pandora said as she stood up, causing Saint's eyes to follow her. Now he was looking up at her as she hovered above, staring down at him.

"You are going to give me what?" Saint said, trying to understand what she was talking about. He was lost.

"My nana," she whispered.

Saint smiled involuntarily, knowing that she meant something other than what she said. He thought about something taboo when he heard the term "nana."

"I think in your country . . . They call it 'pussy,'" Pandora said, now leaving no room for misinterpretation. She said what she fucking said. Pandora turned and walked toward the rear of the room, where a red wooden door was. She had on an oversized spiritual gown, but for the first time, Saint noticed her nice lumps in the back as her wide hips swayed back and forth. Saint watched her closely and was frozen in confusion. He couldn't believe what he had just heard.

"Come on now . . . Do not keep this old woman waiting. It's been many moons since Pandora's box has been opened," she said as she put her hand on the doorknob and slowly peeled her garments off, exposing her shoulders.

Saint didn't know what to say. He was completely caught off guard. He tried to think about what to utter. At first, he wanted to turn it down, but on the other hand, Pandora was a very enticing specimen. He also had never been with an older woman, so the curiosity was most definitely there. *Damn,* he thought to himself as he was stuck standing at a mental crossroad. He then recognized the reality of it and asked himself, *Is Pandora the type of woman you say no to? What the fuck, yo?* He pondered what would be the consequences of doing that. So, he didn't . . .

Saint slowly stood up and watched Pandora's clothes drop to the floor, leaving her completely naked body on full display. Her back was turned toward him as she stood in the doorway with her legs slightly parted. She then took off her head wrap, and long gray locs dropped down liberally. The beautiful hair reached the middle of her back. She ran her hand through them, untangling them and shook her neck, allowing them to drape freely. Her naked, thick but shapely frame was far from what Saint thought it would have been. For a 50-something-year-old woman, her body was amazingly intact. The only indication of her age was the gray hair. The shea butter that was on her body made it shine like no other, and her deep brown skin tone was flawless. Her massive butt cheeks hung down like teardrops, and her thick thighs touched. She knew Saint was watching, so she spread her legs apart a bit more, so her love box was visual from the backside. His mind was blown, seeing that hairy, meaty kitty hanging down so low. It was the plumpest he'd ever seen . . . ever.

"Come get it," she whispered as she slowly disappeared into the dark room.

Saint didn't want to do it, but his manhood had a difference of opinion. He felt the tip of his penis tingle, and shortly after, the whole shaft started to rise. He unhurriedly followed her into the room, and when he walked in, a red light lit the space. After taking two steps in, he stopped in his tracks to admire the seductive scenery. He saw the biggest bed that he ever witnessed sitting in the middle of the room. It was the size of two California King beds put together and was oval-shaped. It looked like a sex den more so than a bedroom. Red silk sheets lined the bed, and a naked Pandora was right in the middle of it. She was lying down while propping herself up on her elbow.

She held her index finger up and signaled for him to come to her. Saint felt like he didn't have control of his legs, and it seemed as if he walked to her against his will. He felt like he floated to her rather than taking steps. The only thing that he could feel was the blood circulating to his dick, which was rock hard.

As he reached the edge of the bed, he took off his shirt and then his pants. He was only left with boxer briefs, and his thick penis print was on full display through the cotton. He stood there with his member bulging and pulsating while looking down at Pandora. His eyes drifted to her big breasts, which were at least a double D in size. Her big brown areoles and nipples were enticing to Saint. She had the type of nipples that, when erect, they stuck straight out like bullets. He glanced at the gray bush between her legs, matching the color of her locs exactly.

He watched as she got on all fours and crawled toward him. Her large breasts were dangling and crashing against each other as she made her way to him. Then she reached over and grabbed him.

"Uhm," she moaned as she rubbed his thick rod through his boxer briefs. She moved her hand up to the elastic waistband of his underwear and slowly peeled them down, making his erect penis pop out like a jack-in-the-box.

"Young bull," she whispered as she held Saint's tool and studied it. His penis tip was plum red because of all of the circulation. A thick, bulging vein ran from the base of his pole, all the way to the beginning of the tip. Saint looked down and watched as it throbbed repeatedly. Pandora took her time and rubbed, jacked, and caressed it. She took her free hand and cupped his sack that was hanging beneath it. She slowly rubbed the sack while stroking his shaft with the other hand. She was using the two-hand action method. Saint threw his head back and closed his eyes, enjoying the masterful job by Pandora.

"You're ready," Pandora confidently said as she lay back and spread her legs. She put her fingers in her mouth and wet them. She then rubbed herself, exposing her chubby lips and swollen area.

Saint climbed onto the bed while never taking his eyes off the prize. He had never before seen a kitty so pudgy and pretty. The contrast of her hair and pink insides was turning him on. Her love box seemed to be raised off of her body like a mound. It was something great to see.

As he climbed onto the colossal bed, he felt like his knees sank into it. It was the softest thing he had ever been on. It was as if he were lying on a bed of clouds, but these clouds were bloodred. She pulled him up, wanting him to straddle her, and brought his penis to her mouth. He followed her lead and waved his manhood over her face as she swallowed him whole. She bobbed her head while grabbing his cheeks, controlling his pace as he stroked her face. Her mouth was so hot and wet as she did work on him. He looked down at her locs and ran his hand through them as she pleased him.

Pandora let out a loud moan of anticipation as she blew him. Saint closed his eyes and listened to her relaxing moans and slurping noises. She hummed and talked nasty in between sucks. Her voice was so clear and coherent in his mind. It seemed as if it were in his head rather than being spoken out loud. He felt like she was speaking to his soul rather than to his eardrums.

All of a sudden, she stopped and looked up at him. Saint locked eyes with her, and it seemed as if he couldn't look away from her gaze. He was stuck . . . mesmerized by her dreamy eyes. She grabbed him and threw him onto his back, swapping positions with him. At that point, she slid down and slowly straddled him. She lined her midsection up with his. Now, she was looking down at him with lustful eyes and freaky intentions. No matter how hard Saint tried, he could not break the eye contact that he was sharing with Pandora. She slightly lifted her ass and reached down to grab his hard tool. Once she found it, she let out a sigh.

"Ooh," she hummed, appreciating how rock solid he was. She then expertly guided him inside of her and sat on him, sliding him deep inside. Saint felt like his pole was diving into a heated Jacuzzi. It was the wettest and warmest that he had ever experienced in his life.

"Hmm," she moaned as she closed her eyes and flickered her tongue.

Saint instantly felt her warm wetness, and her tight womb seemed to grab him. She wildly rode him as her hands slipped down to his neck area. She leisurely tightened her grip, while crashing down onto his pelvis area, riding him like a horse. Her shapely assets waved and jiggled with each thrust. Saint couldn't believe how hard and good this older woman was making love to him.

She plopped her ass up and down, her love box making wet sounds with each crash landing. She rode him with tremendous force and velocity. Her wide hips were moving rapidly. She was on a stern mission to make herself come. She repeatedly raised her big ass and dropped it down on him, making her ass wave like an ocean.

Clap

Clap

Clap

The sounds of lovemaking resonated throughout the room as her cheeks violently plopped down on him, completely soaking his balls. He had never felt a vagina as hot, tight, and wet as Pandora's. It literally felt like heaven on earth. Saint wanted to moan, but he couldn't move. He couldn't speak. He couldn't even move his hands to hold the waist of the beautiful elder on top of him. He was very familiar with that feeling he was experiencing. As a child, he would have similar episodes while in the wee hours of the night. He would wake up with the inability to move or speak. He only could see what was going on around him. He couldn't move anything except his eyeballs from left to right, up and down. Some people called it "A witch riding your back," but that wasn't the case at all . . . a goddess was riding him.

Saint could feel a powerful orgasm coming as Pandora rode him. She could feel hers approaching as well, and she didn't hesitate to tell him.

"Here it comes. Oh my . . . Here it comes," she said as small sweat beads formed on her nose and forehead. Her already firm grip had gotten tighter around Saint's neck, and she kicked it up a notch, riding him like a madwoman.

Saint stared into Pandora's eyes and seemed to get lost in them. He couldn't even blink at that point. Her hazel eyes were the most enticing thing he had ever seen, and he was mystified. He tried to breathe, and he couldn't, but he didn't care.

As the massive orgasm approached, he felt his body stiffen up and the insides of Pandora's vaginal walls contracted. Her walls gripped him tightly, and wet noises emanated from her body. The sounds got louder and louder with each stroke. She had reached her peak and screamed as she released herself. She shook so hard that she quaked his body as well. Her eyes rolled behind her head as her body jerked violently, catching her orgasm. She mumbled under her breath, words that Saint couldn't make out clearly. It was almost as if she were speaking gibberish or in tongues.

At the same exact moment, Saint released his large wad into her and closed his eyes as the sperm shot out of his pole and into her pink abyss. All of a sudden, he felt his entire body being submerged into cold water. The cold sensation sent his body into shock, making him tense up instantly. When he opened his eyes, he saw the brightest blue water around him as he kicked and flailed wildly. It was total confusion. He was literally in the middle of the ocean. He frantically looked around, and his entire scenario had changed within a split second. He was in water kicking and fighting, not being able to wrap his mind around what just happened. Oxygen bubbles came out of his nose and mouth as he looked up and saw the sun shining down through the water.

He instantly swam upward, feeling that he was running out of breath and was about to drown. His heart pounded rapidly, and anxiety ran rapid throughout his chest. So many things were going through his mind as he swam up, confused as ever. His mind was playing tricks on him. He knew that just seconds before, he was under Pandora making love, and now he was submerged in water, trying not to drown.

As he continued to swim, he felt his time was running out, and he would die. At the last second, when he believed that he would pass out from having no air, his head burst out of the water. He felt the hot sun beaming against his face. He took the biggest gasp of air and let the oxygen enter his lungs as he swung his arms wildly, trying to stay afloat.

Ring

Ring

Ring

The alarm clock sounded, waking him up from his dream—or nightmare. He wasn't really sure which one it was. He quickly sat up and looked around frenziedly and realized that he was back in his same hotel room. He looked at the old-fashioned alarm clock, which read 9:04 . . . just like it did in his dream. He reached over to stop it from ringing and then looked down at his body, which was drenched.

"Yo, what the fuck? What the hell was that?" Saint said out loud as he swung his legs over and placed them firmly onto the floor. He looked over and saw the duffle with the bricks of dope, and the feeling of déjà vu overcame him. He had dreamed all his life, so he knew what it felt like. However, that—what he experienced—was *not* a dream.

I wasn't dreaming. I know that for sure, he thought as he stood up and peeled off his drenched clothes. He stood in the middle of the floor naked and then looked down at his morning wood. As he looked closer, he saw something odd. A long strand of hair was on his pelvis. He reached down to grab it and examined it. He held it up so that he could get a better look. He immediately knew that it wasn't his. The hair was gray.

"What the fuck?" he said again as he tried his best to make sense out of what just happened. He proceeded to the bathroom and turned on the shower while shaking his head in confusion.

He stepped in, letting the water cascade down his body. The hot water helped wake him up. The only thing he could think about was his so-called fantasy with Pandora.

It was the best—and worst—dream that he had ever endured. His pipe was still rock hard as if he had a long night of sex. He couldn't stop thinking about the orgasm that he felt. He had never before come that hard, and he was sure that he wasn't fantasizing. It felt too real to him. *How could it be real, and I'm back in the hotel room?* It was all too weird for him, and he was mentally defeated. He chalked it up to his vivid imagination and lack of sleep.

After a few minutes, he stepped out and wrapped himself in a towel. As he stood in front of the mirror, he heard his phone buzz. He looked down at the screen and saw that it was a text from Regis.

Let's have a drink this evening. Talk business . . .

"Same text as in the dream?" Saint asked himself aloud as he frowned. He picked up his phone to reply.

I would love to. But flight chartered to leave in a few hours.

Saint put down his phone after pushing the *send* button. He applied shaving cream on his head to prepare for a shave. To his surprise, Regis immediately shot a text back.

Charter was changed to tomorrow night and upgraded to the G5.

Now, it was just getting outright spooky, and a chill slithered up his spine. He also got goose bumps on his arms as he felt the hairs on the back of his neck stand up. He responded to Regis once again.

Bet.

Saint put down his phone and continued to shave. He instructed Pedro to meet him in the lobby at nine thirty sharp. He sped up the process of shaving, and as he ran the razor across his head, he jumped in pain.

"Fuck," he said under his breath as he turned his head and looked in the mirror to see the damage. He noticed that he had scraped his head and caused blood to trickle from it. He quickly grabbed a piece of tissue and applied pressure to it to stop the bleeding. He couldn't believe what was happening to him as he relived the same steps as the fantasy. He was definitely ready to get out of Cuba and head home, where things weren't so unexplainable. He took care of the scratch and got dressed, grabbed the bricks, and headed over to Pandora's district to see her.

Weird, he thought as he saw the broom upside down, leaning against the wall. He looked down, and the salt was there as well, just like in his fantasy. As he entered the second floor, he made his way back to the room where Pandora was usually waiting. Sage was burning, and smoke danced in the air as he passed through the beaded doorway. Just as he entered, he looked down and saw a puddle of water on the floor, so he immediately stepped over it.

"Hello, Saint," Pandora said with a smile as she sat back at the table.

"Hey, Pandora," he responded, slightly smiling at her.

"Watch that puddle on the floor, baby. You wouldn't want to drown in all that water, now, would you?" she asked rhetorically with a smirk on her face. She winked at him, which made Saint's mind race in curiosity. *Was it real?* he thought to himself as he made his way over to her.

"Is there something different about today . . ." Saint asked as he approached the table, squinting his eyes in confusion. He was trying to figure out if Pandora was playing mind games with him. It seemed as if she knew that he was experiencing déjà vu. He wanted to know if she knew what he had fantasized about.

"Well, it will always be different in this home. Each time you come here, you'll see things differently. My home will always show you what you need to know. What you require will be laid before you. Always," Pandora confirmed with a smile as she started to move her crystals around. Saint carefully placed the bricks on the table as he took in what she said. He remained quiet and just listened carefully.

"Whatever you feel, that's just your ancestors talking to you, so don't be afraid. It's always for your own good," she said with a warm smile. Saint didn't understand what she meant by that; however, he didn't want to ask any more questions. He just wanted to handle his business and leave. That day had been too strange for him as is.

He didn't say much on that particular visit as they went through the ritual with the baptism of the bricks. He left there confused and ready to get back home to the money. However, he had to meet up with Regis later. He wanted to connect with him again. The deep conversation they shared on the flight made him curious about his future plans, outside of the drug game.

Chapter Eight

Snakes

A feast was underway, and lobsters, prawns, and stuffed swordfish were the main dishes. A long table sat on the greenest grass on the private estate owned by Regis. Tall, wicker fire torches were stuck in the ground near the table to provide light as the darkness loomed in the sky. The full moon's light bounced off the ocean, just in front of them as they chowed down. The sounds of the crashing waves created a relaxing ambiance as they gathered. The water wasn't far from them, maybe a few hundred feet from where they sat. Cuban workers moved around the place in white uniforms, serving every need of each guest. Fifty yards behind them stood a large mansion that resembled a palace. Numerous large windows were on the rear of the house, and all of the lights were on, so the elegance of the inside was on full display.

Saint had arrived shortly before and was personally escorted by a car service provided by Regis. Regis had arranged that they pick him up from his hotel once the sun went down. Although Saint had been to Cuba numerous times, he never knew about the modern, beautiful island that he was currently on.

Regis owned the small island on Cuba's soil and used it as a playground for his close friends and business colleagues. It was just off the Atlantic Ocean and sat on a picturesque beach. It only was open when he and his wealthy friends came, so it was a secret to anyone outside of the small town. Regis had flown out a few more friends for that weekend. About twenty-five men congregated, enjoying themselves. The guest list contained nothing but the elitist of the US. Everyone there was affluent with substantial political influence.

Saint was the only nonbillionaire in attendance, and it showed from his silence. However, Saint didn't feel out of place at all. His confidence made him a giant among them. He studied his surroundings, learning more and more with each sidebar conversation he eavesdropped on. He wasn't the only African American in attendance. But by the people's choice of dress and vernacular, he knew that they weren't cut from the same cloth that he was. Saint noticed immediately that their whole swagger was off. They weren't from where he was, and if they were, it had been a very long time since they had been there. He knew that he was the only street guy present, and he liked it that way.

Regis and his friends sat at the table, laughing and drinking the finest Merlot. Saint sat at the table and carefully watched as they talked about the latest stocks and real estate developments that they were a part of. As he heeded attentively, he soon realized that their conversations were different than what he was used to with his crew. They talked about millions as if it were mere dollars. A politician casually mentioned his new hotel in Miami that cost him "300" to develop. Another man at the table bragged about a new erectile dysfunction pill that his team was creating that had cost him "about 50" to produce. Saint instantly knew that the measly million that he had stashed in his floor at home was nothing in their world. Although Saint didn't add to the conversation, he listened and studied while soaking up everything.

Regis sat at the head of the table with his legs crossed, sipping his wine. The elitist of the US would come party with Regis because there were no rules there. No cameras, paparazzi, or bickering wives to be the fun police. He sat there with a shirt, blazer, and ascot on to complement his attire as he was engrossed in the group's conversation. He looked down at the end of the table and noticed that Saint wasn't talking much, so he decided to take the initiative to make him more comfortable.

"Excuse me, gentlemen," Regis said, pardoning himself as he stood up and buttoned his blazer. He looked at Saint and motioned for him to follow him. Saint took his time and wiped off his mouth. Then he stood and walked over.

"Regis," Saint said as he approached him.

"Saint, my guy. How are you enjoying the food?" Regis asked as he casually slid his hands into his white slacks.

"It's delicious. Thanks," Saint answered while walking side by side with him.

"Good. Good. I want you to take a walk with me. I want to show you something," he said as they headed toward the home. They entered, and the inside was truly amazing. It looked like a giant hotel lobby and had big podiums throughout the spacious first floor. Double wraparound stairs with velvet flooring led to the second level.

"So here it is—heaven," Regis said as he opened his arms and slowly spun around, showing off his spot.

"Yeah, this is nice, for sure," Saint said as he looked around and slowly nodded in approval.

"I invited you here because I see something in you. You're a lion. You have an aura about yourself, and I'm very good when it comes to judging character," Regis said as he stepped closer to Saint, looking directly into his eyes.

"I appreciate that. I truly do," Saint said, standing firm and returning the stare. Regis paused for a second and held the gaze, almost like he was sizing Saint up. But, of course, Saint didn't fret.

"Good. You see those men out there?" Regis said as he turned, pointed, and looked at the group fraternizing. He continued, "There is a business connection to anything you want to do in life out there. That's called a power circle. We all look out for one another and build wealth among our faction," Regis explained.

"That's a powerful thing right there," Saint agreed.

"Yes, it is."

"May I ask you something?"

"Sure thing, shoot."

"Well, it's obvious that you know what game I'm in. How can I switch the business? Go legit without having my past catch back up with me?"

"That's a good question. And by asking that, you have separated yourself from the majority of the people in your field. You have bigger aspirations than what you are doing, and that's the key," Regis confirmed. "As I was telling you on the plane, the best thing you can do is make your dirty money, clean," Regis said as he put his hand on Saint's shoulder.

"What's the best way to do that?" Saint asked.

Regis slightly turned Saint so that he could face the outside where the men were. He then pointed.

"See that guy right there in the blue suit? Red hair?" Regis asked as he pointed.

"Yeah."

"That Morris Fillman. He manages one of the biggest investment brokerages in North America."

"Okay," Saint answered as he looked at the dorky-looking, forty-something-year-old man.

"Whatever you give him, he gives half back to you. But when he gives it back, it's via check with his company's logo on it. Clean by way of investment dividends. His brokerage isn't public, so there's no way authorities can verify or double-check your numbers. Voilà . . . clean money to live and do with what you please," Regis explained as simple as he could.

"Oh, I see," Saint answered.

"Then after that, you give him that same check, and you sit back and watch him work his magic. You think moving dope is lucrative? That's peanuts compared to the stock market . . . if done right," Regis clarified.

"Well, I need to talk to him. We need to do some business together."

"Agreed. But he's real timid. You have to ease your way in with him. Take on some of his interests and then approach him with it. For instance, he's a heavy gambler. You talk gambling, and he will talk your ear off all night," Regis said, chuckling, showing his perfect, fake, porcelain teeth.

"Oh yeah?" Saint said.

"Oh, for sure. That's why he's here now. He doesn't drink. Doesn't fuck around on his wife. No drugs . . . nothing. He's here for the dogfighting. He bets a million a match," Regis explained.

"We used to fight dogs back in my hood . . ." Saint paused, correcting himself, knowing that Regis wouldn't understand his slang. He continued, "We used to fight dogs back in my old neighborhood when I was young."

"No disrespect, but this dogfighting is not like what you are used to. This is a whole different monster. High stakes like you wouldn't even imagine."

"Is that right?"

"Yeah, this is my group of friends. But there are many groups like us around the world, and one thing that all men have in common, no matter the country . . . All men are competitive. So, once a month, we meet here and fight our dogs. That's one of the unspoken main attractions in Cuba."

"Okay, I can fuck with that for sure," Saint said.

"We actually are having one tonight, if you want to come."

"One tonight?" Saint asked.

"Yeah, an old-fashioned dogfight. A few times a year, we have an event and show who's boss. Every team brings their pick of the litter and throws them in the ring."

"Yeah, I'm game. I'm down."

"Great. I have a bitch that hasn't lost in two years. She's a vicious li'l fucker too. She kills whatever I put in front of her," Regis boasted. "Then it's set. We have a few hours before that starts, so let's have fun in the meantime," he suggested.

"Cool."

"Follow me," Regis instructed as he walked further into the home. They made a quick right, and Saint saw an extremely long, narrow corridor before them. The hallway was nearly pitch dark. If not for the candles that were lit along the walls, they wouldn't be able to see. He noticed that there was a line of doors on each side of the hall. It began to make sense to Saint.

This was an old, converted hotel, he thought, as the row of doors were lined up against the wall. Regis walked to the first door and then looked back, smiling at him. As he opened the door, he stepped aside so Saint could peek in.

"Have a look-see," Regis instructed as he nodded his head in the direction of the room. Saint stepped forward and peered inside. The room was dimly lit. He was taken off guard by what he was observing. A tall, slender woman wearing an all-leather catsuit stood there with a whip in hand. She wore six-inch heels and looked like an Amazonian. She had long, blond hair and wore bright red lipstick. A naked, pale, white man was standing up with ropes tied to each limb, stretching him out. He looked like a standing starfish. A black gag ball was in his mouth, and red whip marks covered his body. His ass was as red as an apple from an obvious beating, and the sight alone made Saint cringe. Loud, heavy metal music played as the woman wearing leather cracked the whip against his backside, causing a loud slapping noise to erupt through the air. The woman shot a look at the door and noticed Saint.

"Get your ass in here, you little bitch," she said to Saint as she cracked her whip in the air, making a loud, snapping noise. She then ran her tongue across her top lip seductively.

"What the fuck?" Saint said under his breath as he was in unfamiliar territory. Regis saw that he was uncomfortable, so he quickly pulled the door shut.

"Don't worry. We have a room for everyone. Apparently, that wasn't your cup of tea," Regis said as he headed to the next door. He continued to talk to Saint as they made their way down the hall. "This is the place that every man dreams of. A buffet of whatever you like to do. Gambling, sex, drugs . . . They're all here. Whatever your twist is, there's a door for you."

"Y'all got some wild shit going on in this mu'fucka," Saint said, smiling, as he tried to wrap his mind around the whole experience.

"Trust me, the older you get and the more money you accumulate . . . your sexual pallet broadens. The more powerful you become, the bigger your appetite," Regis explained.

He stopped at the next door and opened it. Saint was hesitant about looking in, not knowing what he would see on the other side of the door. Regis stepped aside once again, making a clear path for Saint. Saint stepped in and saw a bed of women of mixed ethnic backgrounds in an all-out orgy. They looked like a pile of snakes how they were all intertwined with one another. Fake breasts, long hair, and different skin tones were everywhere. They were all in the bed, sucking each other and tribbing. “Tribbing” was a term used when two women rubbed their clitoris against each other while scissoring. Masturbation, moaning, and strap-on dildos were all in the human gumbo.

Saint couldn’t focus on one particular thing because so much was going on. Sweaty bodies were thrusting against one another, and wet noises were rampant. Seven different women touched and pleased each other, and Saint liked what he saw. However, he didn’t want to indulge. Although it did look enticing, the thought of the dream that he experienced earlier had him encouraged to stay faithful to Ramina.

Cuba be on that bullshit, Saint thought, as he remembered the last time that he tried to get some pussy, he ended up in an ocean. *Won’t get me this time,* he thought to himself and smiled at his own inside joke.

He was there to get a plug, not get off track. He wasn’t searching for something new. He wanted a plug to the good life outside of the streets.

“I’m good,” Saint said as he stepped out of the room. Regis looked in confusion as he stepped back, boggled. It was very rare that a man didn’t give in to his sexual desires—especially when it was presented on a silver platter.

“Ooh, I see. You like what *I* like,” Regis said as he smiled widely and pointed his finger at Saint as if he had him figured out.

Regis walked back to the main area where they were before. He then put two of his fingers in his mouth and whistled so loudly that it made Saint's ears ring. Saint looked in puzzlement, not knowing what Regis was doing. But he would soon find out.

A few seconds later, a door opened on the second floor. Then out walked a beautiful young girl with long, flowing hair and an olive skin-colored complexion.

Saint's eyes followed Regis's, and they both watched as the girl with lacy lingerie came down the stairs. As she got closer, Saint felt immoral. She looked extremely too young to be in the presence of grown men. As she stood before them, Saint was sure that the girl was underage. Her body hadn't even fully developed yet. Her breasts were only nubs, and they barely filled the lingerie. She basically didn't have any. Her small frame didn't make it any better. She looked like a baby. She hadn't even developed womanly hips yet. Saint instantly grew uncomfortable and looked away, not wanting to look at a young girl that way. From his estimate, she had to be around 14, and that was a no-go for him.

"Hey, sunshine," Regis said as he cupped her face and pecked her on the forehead.

"Hey, papi," she answered as she avoided eye contact with him.

"Tay, I want you to meet our friend," Regis said as he placed his hand on the small of her back.

Saint looked at her and noticed that she wore heavy makeup. But he could still see the bruises underneath, obviously trying to be concealed. He looked at the skinny girl, and instantly his heart dropped, feeling sorry for her. Tattoos covered her body, and it made her look tomboyish. However, she was still was a pretty girl. Her long, curly hair and captivating light eyes gave her an exotic island look. Saint immediately knew that she was of Cuban descent by her features. Regis didn't fly her in like he did the rest of the girls. This was his local guilty pleasure.

"Hello, mister," Tay said as she looked up at Saint. Saint nodded his head at her and gave a half grin. He instantly started to second-guess his new friendship with Regis.

"Nah, I don't like what you like," Saint said through his clenched teeth as he looked at Regis with a piercing glare. His anger was too much to hide, and it was spilling out.

"Don't knock it 'til you try it," Regis said, not catching on to Saint's disgust for his choice of sexual indulgence. He looked down at Tay and then grabbed his crotch, thinking about what he would do later.

"Go back up to the room. We will continue this after the dogfight," he said as he rubbed her bangs from her face.

"Yes, daddy," Tay said timidly as she smiled. Saint could tell that the youngster was terrified, and it really bothered him. He wasn't a saint, but he didn't believe in pedophilia in no way, shape, or form.

"I can get you one of those delivered like a package," Regis said with a grin on his face.

"What do you mean?" Saint asked, not fully understanding Regis's statement.

"I can have one of those straight to your door. A live-in nanny that's open and willing to do whatever, whenever you want. All of her papers and green card would be legit and taken care of by my connections. They're like little lapdogs. Will be indebted to you just for getting them out of this hellhole country. Trust me," Regis explained.

Saint's insides were burning up in anger. He had a soft spot for things like that because of his mother. She was a victim of human trafficking in her past. Her former drug addiction put her into situations that she regretted every day. The stories that she told him broke his heart, and he immediately recalled those talks with his mom. When he saw Tay, he saw his mother. He immediately thought about the rise of young girls being human trafficked and how he despised it.

He watched as Tay walked away and knew that he would have to bite his tongue in the presence of this circle. He was sharp enough to understand not to offend people in positions of power. Although he didn't say anything, he knew that would be the last time he visited Regis's resort.

Chapter Nine

God of Dog

It had been a few hours since Saint had seen the young girl, and it still bothered him. He followed the group of men who were all mostly drunk and belligerent as they headed toward the elevators at the end of the hall. More guests had come in via helicopter, and the stage was set. It was time for the dogfight.

Multiple elevators lined up at the end of the hall as the men waited their turn to pile in. Everyone was itching to get to the basement level. Regis explained to Saint that he had created an underground arena where the fights took place. Throughout the night, Regis had introduced Saint to so many men that were willing and open to connect with him when he returned home. Not to mention a federal judge, who told Saint that if he ever needed any favors not to hesitate and call Regis, so it could "get taken care of." Saint's mind was blown at the networks that were made. However, the sight of young children was something that he could not shake.

As the group of men piled into the elevator, Saint noticed that the tension was high, and excitement permeated the air. Everyone was eager to see the fight. Saint couldn't understand how a dogfight could be so electric. It was unlike anything that he had ever seen.

Regis stood next to Saint as they watched the elevator doors close. Moments later, the elevator descended.

Once they reached the bottom floor, the doors opened, and when they parted, Saint's mind overwhelmed at what he saw. The chaotic, roaring sound of people filled the air and felt like a zoo. People were yelling, bantering, and waving money in the air like they were in a sports stadium. The atmosphere reminded him of a World Cup soccer game only smaller. It was so intense. The ground wasn't finished and was made of brown dirt and dust. It looked as if they were in a supersized bomb shelter. Lanterns lined the red clay walls and provided lights for the grimy venue.

"What the fuck?" Saint said as he stepped into the underground fight club.

Everyone stood in a gigantic circle and were taking bets with one another, awaiting the event to start. Regis leaned over and explained to Saint what was going on. The hot, humid smell of musty men was pungent, and the air was thick.

"This event is open to the locals to come to watch and bet. I had a private elevator installed that connects my estate. As you can see, this arena runs through the entire downtown Havana. This is what everyone is here for. Millions are won or lost right here," Regis explained as they squeezed in and joined the crowd. Saint nodded his head as he listened carefully.

A bell rang, and a short, chubby Cuban man emerged from the middle of the crowd. The crowd cheered and raved when he stood with both of his hands in the air. He then stepped onto a soapbox that was in the midst of the gigantic circle of men. He fanned his hands in a downward motion, signaling for people to calm down so that he could speak.

"Welcome . . . welcome . . . welcome," he yelled with a heavy Spanish accent. The crowd went crazy in anticipation as he waved his hands, once again signaling for them to quiet down.

"Coming from Santiago de Cuba, Luca Bazooka," the short man yelled as he looked to the corner of the room. Saint's eyes shot to the corner as well so that he could see what type of dog was being brought out. However, he didn't see any animal. Instead, he saw a young boy coming out as his trainer followed him massaging his shoulders. As Saint looked closely, he saw that the boy looked familiar. It was the young boy that he had given his chain to when he first arrived. The young boy still had on the golden chain with the saint on the charm, so that confirmed it.

"What's going on?" he said under his breath as he watched the boy walk past him and into the middle of the people.

Luca shadowboxed as he stood there, shirtless and shoeless. He swung wildly. There was obviously no real skill there. Anyone with sense could see that Luca was untrained. He wore raggedy, stained, and soiled jean shorts. They were the same ones that he had on when Saint had seen him before. That's when Saint understood that the "dogs" that Regis mentioned were, in fact, kids. They were running an underground kids' fight club. While everyone was ranting and raving, Saint just watched, shaking his head. The next fighter was introduced, and he got a warm ovation as well. The young boy came out and was much bigger than Luca. They didn't waste any time. The fight began.

The older boy immediately pummeled Luca. He delivered crushing blows, one after another. His fist seemed to touch every part of Luca's skull. Luca didn't even attempt to dodge or block any of the punches. He just swung wildly, giving it his all trying to fight back. Nonetheless, it was no match. Saint cringed and jumped at every vicious punch thrown at Luca. To see kids brawling like that was sickening to his stomach. After the boy beat Luca into a fetal position, he started stomping on him. Saint looked at the short Cuban man, thinking that he would stop the fight because, surely, it was over. But nothing happened. The men just cheered and hollered like barbarians.

"Stop the fucking fight," Saint said as he looked at the Cuban. The larger boy continued to stump on Luca's head, and blood oozed out of his mouth. "Stop the fight, mu'fucka!" Saint yelled as he stepped forward. Regis grabbed Saint's arm and pulled him back.

"It's to the death, son. Relax," Regis said. Saint snatched his arm away from Regis and gave him a stern stare. Regis then looked at the Cuban man and gave him a signal. Regis motioned his hand across his neck, signaling him to stop the fight. The short Cuban man instantly grabbed the bigger fighter and waved his arm, indicating that it was over. The crowd erupted as the Cuban raised the right hand of the boy, crowning him the victor.

Immediately, a man came, assisting Luca, and dragged him to the back. Saint watched as he shook his head in repulsion. He looked at the ground and saw that his chain had fallen off of Luca during the fight, so he quickly picked it up and examined it. He flipped it over and saw his initials on it.

They treated li'l homie like he was a dog. This ain't right, man, Saint thought to himself. He looked around and noticed that no one seemed to be bothered by the child abuse that was going on. They traded money. Some were cheering. Others were mad because of their loss. Saint stepped back next to Regis as he was conversing with an older Asian man that Saint hadn't noticed before. He listened closely as they exchanged words.

"Okay, so put your money where your mouth is," Regis yelled at the man. He then proceeded to light a cigar that was in between his index finger and thumb. He took a deep pull, and a bright orange ring of fire formed at the tip. Regis was very confident with his words as he didn't give the man the respect of looking at him as he spoke. The Asian man calmly whispered something to Regis. Regis nodded his head and said simply, "Bet."

The bell rang once again, and the crowd became antsy. The man stepped onto the soapbox once more and announced the second set of fighters.

"Next, we have Big Papi . . . the Spanish Bruiser," the short Cuban man said as he threw his hand in the direction of the fighter who emerged from the crowd. Saint looked at the young boy who was nearly six feet tall and seemed to be in his early teens. He was a full-blooded Cuban and had strong facial features. His bulging muscles didn't match his innocent, adolescent, baby face. The crowd erupted in jeers as the bruiser cracked his neck by stretching it from side to side. He then flexed his muscles, making each one of his pectorals bounce up and down. He was a beast.

Regis grabbed Saint and whispered in his ear. "Here comes my champion. Watch this," he said. On cue, the Cuban man introduced the next contender.

"Now, we have the fighter who everyone has been waiting on. The lady of the night . . . Tay . . . the Cubana."

The crowd erupted and chanted in unison . . .

"Cubana!"

"Cubana!"

"Cubana!"

The bell for the elevator chimed, and all eyes shot in its direction. Out came Tay, the same underage girl that Saint saw earlier wearing the sexy lingerie. This time, she wore shorts and a sports bra, exposing her tattooed body. Tay had different animals tatted on her body, which blended flawlessly. Lions, snakes, beautiful birds, and bears were all a part of her colorful collage. Her small frame was without any fat. The only thing that had any meat was her plump buttocks. Her breasts were nonexistent, and her long hair was pulled back neatly, showing her soft baby hairs that rested on her edges.

"That's my li'l bitch I was telling you about," Regis said proudly as she walked into the circle of men.

"Wait—she's about to fight that big mu'fucka?" Saint asked in confusion as he noticed the drastic difference in size.

"Don't let the size fool you. Tay is a boy at heart. She has a fire inside of her. She's a fucking animal. Watch this," Regis said confidently. Saint watched as Tay squared up and never took her eyes off of her opponent. Her fists were up, protecting her face as she shifted her weight from left to right, slowly rocking. Tay was laser-focused as she sized him up.

Saint couldn't believe what he was seeing. *I know they're not about to let this little girl fight this big-ass nigga,* Saint thought as he remained quiet and observed. He clenched his jaws down tightly and tried his best to bite his tongue and not speak up. With people feverishly placing bets with one another, it resembled the New York Stock Exchange.

Another bell rang, and the fight commenced. Tay strategically circled the bruiser, who was twice her size, slowly stalking him. The bruiser let out a roaring yell as he tried to attack her with a bear hug.

"Aaargh," he yelled as he lunged at her.

Tay swiftly ducked, and he missed terribly, catching nothing but the air in his attempt. Saint instantly realized that she was light and quick on her feet. Her footwork was amazing. It was a far cry from what he saw with Luca. The bruiser got noticeably frustrated and tried again. But this time, Tay stepped to the side and held out her foot, tripping him. He instantly fell flat on his face. A cloud of dust rose as he crashed on the ground. As he tried to get up, Tay caught him with a hard right fist to the jaw. Her ferociousness surprised Saint, and he watched the blood trickle from the bruiser's mouth. She then followed up with another one that sent him flying back onto the dust flat on his back. The crowd praised her. Tay stepped back and let him get up. When he stood, he staggered slightly. It was evident that he was disorientated.

Tay quickly ran up to him and threw a quick uppercut to the gut, making him double over in pain. She promptly caught him with a knee to the face, sending him flying onto his back once again. The audience went into a frenzy. Hoots and hollers filled the air as Tay stood over him and breathed deeply. Her chest moved up and down rapidly. It looked as if she had a baboon was in her chest cavity, trying to get out.

"That's right. That's Daddy's girl," Regis yelled and clapped his hands.

Tay looked over at Regis, and it was the first time that Saint had seen her smile. Tay immediately lit up, knowing that she had made Regis proud. She was so into Regis clapping for her that she didn't see her opponent rise. Regis's smile quickly turned upside down as he looked past her, seeing the bruiser raise his fist. Tay saw the change of expression on Regis's face and turned around. But by then, it was too late. The boy came hard down across her temple with a fierce elbow, causing her to fall on the ground. The crowd gasped in harmony as the loud thud echoed throughout the place. Tay tried to get up but was quickly met with a fierce kick to her head. It didn't stop there. The boy repeatedly kicked her in the stomach, face, and then back. He stumped her out, beating her to a pulp, and Saint grew uncomfortable seeing the girl being abused like that. He looked at Regis and urged him to stop the fight.

"Stop this, man," he calmly said as he couldn't stand the sight anymore.

Regis was so infuriated that he would lose the million-dollar bet that he just gritted his teeth and remained silent.

"Stop the fucking fight," Saint said again, this time with more anger and aggression.

Regis looked at the short Cuban and made a gesture, angrily waving his hand across his neck. Immediately, the Cuban grabbed the bruiser, and just like that, the bout was over. Some people were cheering, while others were sulking in defeat. After a few moments of bickering, the place cleared out. Regis watched as the people walked past him and shook their heads in disbelief. Saint stood there alongside him until it was mostly empty. Tay was still on the ground, trying to gather herself. Regis looked at her with hatred and shook his head just before storming out toward the elevators. Saint watched as he exited and then focused his attention on Tay. He went over to help her up, seeing that she needed assistance. It seemed like no one cared that a girl just got her ass handed to her.

"Let me help you up," he said as he kneeled and assisted her to her feet.

"Thank you," she said as she wiped the blood from her mouth. To Saint, it started to make sense about why she had bruises under her makeup. She was a street fighter.

"Are you okay?" he asked.

"Yes, I'm good. He just caught me with a lucky punch. It was my fault," she said in disappointment as she dropped her head in defeat.

"He was twice your size. You shouldn't have been fighting him, to begin with. That was some bullshit. Shouldn't even be fighting a dude. You're a fuckin' girl. Doesn't make sense," Saint said, not understanding how the men could be so cold.

"You don't understand this world," Tay said while looking Saint in the eyes. She realized that it was his first time in this underground thing of theirs. Most wouldn't understand the inner workings of that realm.

"How old are you?" Saint asked as he helped her to the stool in the far corner.

"I'm 17," she answered.

"You look like a baby. Didn't even think you were that old," he said, looking at her undeveloped body. His eyes wandered to her arms, and that's when he noticed the many track marks. He had been in the heroin game for a long time, and he knew what needle marks looked like when he saw them. He immediately understood that she did dope. "You're still too young to be involved in shit like this," he said, not wanting to believe her strife.

"Yeah, but I have been fighting all of my life. Nothing new," she answered.

"Why do you do this? Where are your parents?" he asked, trying to get a better understanding of how she ended up in a predicament like the one she was in.

"I don't have parents. Never have."

"Damn—"

Before Saint could say anything else, another Cuban girl emerged from the elevator and yelled something to Tay in Spanish. Tay instantly replied to her and then looked at Saint.

"Listen, I have to go get dressed and get ready for tonight." With that, she hurried to meet the girl and left Saint in the cave alone.

The current trip to Cuba had been crazy, and he was ready to get out of Dodge to get back to some type of normalcy.

Chapter Ten

Straight Flush

It was nearing four a.m., and guests were still at Regis's place. Everyone was in the estate's poker room, sitting at various tables gambling. Things had died down since the dogfight earlier that night. Regis and a few of his closest friends, including Morris Fillman, were at one table playing Texas Hold'em at $50,000 a hand. Cuban dealers sat at different tables, conducting the high-stakes poker games. Regis had it set up like a real casino—only it was in his place. Saint had never seen anything like it before.

Half-naked women walked around in lingerie, serving them cocktails, drugs, and blow jobs on command. Saint played the back and watched as the billionaires freaked off, going in and out of the random rooms. They would gamble and then go get their freak on . . . gamble . . . then freak. That cycle was ongoing all night. Saint only sipped Cognac and observed, deciding not to indulge. He played a few hands of poker on and off but didn't go overboard. He only played enough not to look like an outsider and blend in more easily. He sat and watched Regis lose north of $300,000 during that one sitting. Saint instantly realized that Regis had a bad gambling problem. Saint was sitting behind Regis, so he saw the hands that were played. Saint witnessed Regis go all-in on hands that he had no business doing so on. Regis was a reckless risk taker, and it was easy to see. Saint witnessed him lose hand after hand, just being frivolous with his money. Saint also noticed something else. The dealer was dealing from the bottom of the deck, always being in favor of Morris Fillman. They were cheating, but Saint minded his own business on that matter.

Saint's mind was elsewhere. The underage kids fighting was weighing heavy on him, and he couldn't shake the guilt of knowing and not doing anything about it. Also, the sight of needle tracks on the young girl's arm was constantly replaying in his thoughts. Saint's mother battled with addiction, and she explained how her pimp would use the drug to control her and to keep her needing him. He knew Tay was in a similar situation.

He looked around and couldn't understand how these grown men just overlooked the bullshit that was taking place on their watches. He wanted to speak his mind and leave, but he knew it was chess and not checkers. He couldn't look down on a room full of billionaires and not expect to make powerful enemies. Enemies in that room could be dangerous. Very dangerous, indeed. That was something he did not need in the line of work that he was in. So, he decided to play it cool and leave when everyone else did. But by the way things were looking, they would be there until the sun rose. The cocaine had everyone up and lively as if it were in the middle of the afternoon.

Saint saw Tay enter the room wearing a skimpy red nightgown and had a face full of makeup, attempting to cover her war wounds from earlier that night. He watched as she walked over to Regis while he continued to play cards. He had a fat Cuban cigar sticking out of the right side of his mouth.

"Hey, daddy," Tay said as she smiled and approached him. She placed her hand on his shoulder.

"You lost me one million dollars. Do you know that?" he said, not even giving her the respect of looking at her.

"I'm so sorry, daddy. I should—" Tay said in a shaky voice. It was evident that she was terrified because it was written all over her face. Regis put his hand up to signal her to hush, and she did immediately midsentence.

"I don't want to hear your fuckin' excuses," Regis responded as he studied his cards. The disappointment was all over Tay's face as the words killed her softly.

"I won't lose again. I'm so sorry," Tay pleaded as her eyes watered. She had a lot at stake when dealing with Regis. He provided her with a roof over her head. The thought of her being homeless and walking the streets of Havana again was terrifying. She had been staying at the estate for a while. It was her only home. Going back to the streets was an unbearable thought. Fear set in, and Tay's tears started to flow. Being desperate, she got down on her knees and clasped her hands in a begging position. She sat at his feet with her head down, like she was a small dog. Saint looked around and couldn't believe no one else was bothered by this.

"You know how to make this better?" he said as he looked down at her.

"Anything . . ." she said as she looked up with optimistic eyes.

"Blow every single person at this table," he instructed as he pointed to the four others around the table.

"Okay, I'll do anything," she said without hesitation as she wiped the tears away.

Regis looked down at her and forcefully grabbed her face. "At the same time," he added with a sick smile. He was getting enjoyment out of treating her like a filthy animal, and it was evident. Regis looked at his poker hand and tossed the cards into the center of the table, losing again.

"Fuck," he said under his breath. "This bitch is bad luck." He stood up and said, "Go in the red room and wait for everyone. They'll show you not to showboat while fighting again." Tay nodded her head in agreement and hurried out. Saint was disgusted as his eyes followed Tay as she walked away.

The men laughed and talked about the nasty things that they were going to do with her. Saint had seen enough. He had to do something.

"Hey, I want that dirty bitch," he said as he grabbed his crotch and rubbed himself through his pants. Saint ran his tongue over his perfect teeth and stood at the table.

"Excuse me?" Regis said as he looked at Saint in confusion. Saint was mostly quiet through the night, so it was a big surprise to everyone that he had said what he said.

"You heard me. I want the li'l dirty bitch," Saint repeated as he stood at the table.

"That's my boy. I *knew* you would come around. I was starting to think something was wrong with you," Regis lightheartedly said just before he puffed his cigar. Everyone at the table laughed. Saint put on a fake smile, but his blood was boiling on the inside. He hated to even talk in that manner, but he had to. He couldn't see the abuse go any further. He had to play their game.

"Cool, well, you can go in with everyone else. She can handle one more. Trust me," Regis responded.

"Nah, I want that bitch to myself. I want that nanny situation," Saint said, going with the flow, climbing deeper into the belly of the beast. It was as if the words flowed out without him wanting them to. For some reason, he just felt like he was supposed to save her. He felt the responsibility of making sure that she was okay. It was like nothing else that he ever felt before.

"You freaky motherfucker," Regis said as he pointed his finger at Saint and waved it while smiling widely.

"I knew it," Morris Fillman said as he smiled from ear to ear, seemingly being relieved that Saint was a part of their pedophilia ring.

"She's damaged goods anyway. The bitch is bad luck. So, if you want her . . . you got her. Papers and birth certificate saying she's 21. Green card. All of that will be taken care of. She can fly back with you on the private. No TSA . . . no trouble. Easy breezy," Regis said as if he had done it hundreds of times before. That was because he had.

"Play for her—one hand. A million," Saint said boldly as he looked directly in Regis's eyes. Regis paused and stared at Saint to see if he was serious. He studied him closely. It seemed like something clicked, and he was instantly game.

"Easy. Let's do it," Regis responded as he rubbed his hands together. The adrenaline rush of high-stakes gambling excited him to his core.

Saint grabbed Morris on his shoulder and gave him a very firm squeeze and said sternly, "I want this seat. I like the luck this spot has," he said as he stared a hole through Morris's eyes while keeping a firm squeeze. Saint then looked at the dealer with the same gaze, letting him know that he was up on their deceitful hustle. Saint didn't say anything to them verbally about it, but they both understood that their underhandedness had been exposed. Their hands were tied. They knew that they had to play along or potentially get outed as cheaters. Morris stood up, and Saint sat down, taking his place. Saint rubbed his hands together and clapped twice.

"Let's get it," he said excitedly.

"Okay, so the bet is one hand. One million, correct?" Regis confirmed.

"That's right. I want to take the bitch home," Saint said with fake excitement.

"Before we start . . . You know what you're getting, right? I just want to be clear," Regis said. Saint instantly knew that Regis was referring to the girl's age, which was illegal. He assumed Regis was just giving him a warning before he stepped into the ring of pedophilia. Once a member . . . always a member.

"Yeah, I know," Saint answered.

They were dealt their hand, and needless to say, Saint easily won with a straight flush. He had won the rights to Tay. However, Saint didn't know what he was getting himself into. But after that night, his life would *never* be the same.

Never.

Saint walked into the red room and saw Tay sitting on the bed with her head down. He closed the door behind him and locked it so that no one would come in. He walked over to her, and she immediately attempted to drop to her knees to give him a blow job. Saint caught her by her elbows and lifted her.

"No . . . no. Stop. You don't have to do that," he said as he stood her to her feet. He took a deep breath and shook his head, feeling sorry for her.

"What do you mean?" she said, not understanding why Saint denied her.

"I mean, you don't have to do any of this anymore. I'm getting you out of here."

"What are you talking about? I belong to Regis."

"No, not anymore. You don't belong to him or any of them other mu'fuckas. You're getting out of here," Saint said as he reached into his pockets and pulled out a wad of money. "Here, take this and get yourself together."

Tay took the money and looked at it. "Regis will have me killed. I don't think you understand how things work in this country."

"Listen, li'l mama, this isn't normal. This isn't the way it's supposed to be. Them mu'fuckas up there are sick. I can't make you leave, but I can give you a way out," he explained. Tay's eyes watered. She had never met any man that hadn't tried to use or abuse her. Her parents abandoned her, and Regis was the only person that had ever shown her any interest. She didn't know there was another way, and now this complete stranger was trying to help her. She was confused, overwhelmed, and grateful, all at the same time.

"I used to be on the streets selling my body. Regis came and saved me," Tay admitted, beginning to feel bad and ungrateful. A classic case of Stockholm syndrome.

"He didn't save you. He preyed on you. Why don't you understand that? You're a child still. Your mind hasn't even fully developed yet," Saint said, shaking his head. "Fuck that . . . You're coming with me," he said. His heart wouldn't let her stay.

"Okay . . . okay," she said as she cried. Somehow, she could see in Saint's eyes that he had good intentions.

"But how? Regis will come after me."

"No . . . No, he won't. You're free. I made sure of that. He thinks you're coming with me back home," Saint explained.

"Home, with you?"

"Well, I'm not taking you. I just said that so I could get you away from him."

"Are you serious? He let me go?" Tay asked.

"Yeah, dead-ass serious. You're not his property anymore. You got to get the fuck out of here. Can't you just go home? Where's the rest of your family?" Saint quizzed.

"Cuba is different. They disowned and threw me away. You wouldn't understand," Tay said as the tears welled up in her eyes.

"Fuck . . ." Saint said under his breath after realizing he didn't have a plan. His heart made him react, and now, he might have put her in a worse position than she already was. "You can just come with me. We can figure something out. But this . . . this ain't it."

"I can go with you?" Tay asked as she looked up at Saint. Saint nodded yes, not knowing what he was getting himself into. He just followed his heart, and his heart led him straight back to the bayou . . . with Tay.

Chapter Eleven

Wolves

"Y'all mu'fuckas better line up, or ain't shit moving," Zoo said as he sat on the stoop eating a bag of sunflower seeds.

Dope fiends were scattered around the house as they waited for the shop to open. A few of the wolves were standing behind Zoo. "Wolves" are what he called his street crew and the young hustlers who ran the dope houses. As soon Zoo made the announcement, the fiends got in line, anxiously waiting on their turn to get served.

"Gunner, open up shop," Zoo instructed as he looked back at the young hustler who wore short dreadlocks that were wild all over his head.

Gunner stood just under six feet and was chiseled. He was a young man but moved with an old soul. He had a caramel complexion and broad shoulders. He was one of the few that spoke to Saint personally. Zoo had taken him under his wing, and he knew that he would be the next one up. The only thing stopping him was his young age. But everyone knew that when Gunner got older, he would be strong in the streets. The work that he had put in for Zoo was legendary. Gunner had a long scar on his face that was barely noticeable. It ran from his earlobe to his chin and had a very dark story behind it. As Gunner served the fiends their morning fix, a white Rover pulled up on to the block. He immediately knew it was Saint.

Saint would always pull up but never get out to the spots. Zoo looked over at him and nodded his head, acknowledging him. Saint flashed his lights in response. Zoo got back to business and watched their money getting made. He pulled out a bag of weed and placed it on a book that was on the porch. Then he broke down the buds.

As the fiends came and copped their packs one by one, Gunner took the money. Then he sent them two houses down where another worker was distributing packs. Their operation was a well-oiled machine and intricate. Fiends would give Gunner the money, and he would hold up his hand to signal how many packs they bought. The lookout across the street would then signal to the worker two houses down. After that, the fiends would walk down to get served. The money and the dope were completely separated.

Gunner looked at the young man who had a small Afro and raggedy clothes who was up next in line. Gunner always felt bad when he saw him because he was too young to be a dope fiend. He didn't look a day older than 18, and he walked with a feminine bop. His eyebrows were arched, and his nails were always painted. His hand gestures were feminine. He couldn't help it. It was just who he was. The humble young man went by the name of Cooda.

"Cooda, I thought you were done with this shit, man. Didn't you just get out of rehab?" Gunner playfully said as Cooda held out a wrinkled twenty-dollar bill.

"Man, you know that shit doesn't work. I did that to complete my drug program," he admitted as he showed his gap-toothed smile.

"Oh yeah, you did get picked up the other week, didn't you?"

"Stealing copper out of them HUD homes," one of the wolves said, making some of the others burst out in laughter.

"Ol' zesty ass," another small-framed wolf added. They all got a good laugh off of Cooda's feminine ways. Zoo listened without saying anything but figured he'd heard enough. He saw that Cooda looked uncomfortable and embarrassed.

"All right, y'all better leave Cooda alone. Didn't he whoop off in yo' ass last summer for talking shit about him being gay? Better chill out before he gives yo' ass a round two," Zoo said with a smirk on his face.

"Ooh yeah, I forgot about that," somebody said as they laughed even louder, remembering when Cooda had enough of the bullying and put hands on the small-framed hustler.

The small hustler didn't like the fact that everyone was laughing at him. Cooda smiled and shook his head, not wanting to stir up old stuff. The smirk was too much for the wolf, so he went over to Cooda and shoved him off of the porch, sending him flying backward. The back of Cooda's head hit the grass as he dropped hard. The wolf then pulled out his gun and hopped off the porch. He walked over to Cooda, stood over him, and pointed his gun at the boy's head.

"Fuck you laughing at, faggot-ass nigga?" he asked, feeling humiliated.

Saint quickly hit his horn, and everyone's attention went toward his car.

"A'ight, that's enough," Zoo said as he licked the leaf that his weed was rolled in. He stood up and brushed the weed remnants off his fresh gray jogging suit. He put the rolled blunt in his mouth and reached out his hand and helped Cooda up. Cooda grabbed his hand and stood up. He then brushed the grass off the back of his head.

"Yo, Cooda, you still know how to hook up cable?" Zoo said, feeling bad for him.

"Yeah, big homie. I can do it," Cooda answered.

"Bet. Stop by the shop sometime this week and hook me up. I be needing to watch SportsCenter while I'm in that mu'fucka late at night," Zoo said.

"Bet," Cooda replied as he smiled through the pain that was in his lower back from the fall. Zoo looked over to Gunner and said, "This one's on me." Gunner nodded and held up a signal to the guy across the street.

"Gon' 'head and get right. Don't forget to stop by the shop later," Zoo reminded Cooda as he lit his weed.

"Thanks, Zoo," Cooda said as his face lit up. He stuffed the twenty in his pocket and headed down to cop his drugs.

Zoo looked down the block and blew out weed smoke. "Y'all niggas hold it down. I'll be back later to check the count," he said before heading over to Saint's car.

"Peace, beloved," Saint said as Zoo took a seat on his passenger side.

"Peace," Zoo said as he reached over and slapped hands with his right-hand man.

"How we looking?" Saint asked.

"Just opened up shop for the day. But yesterday, we killed 'em. Ran through the whole thang at this spot. Had to go uptown and take from that pack just to make sure we didn't run out again," Zoo explained.

"Good. Good," Saint said as he checked his rearview mirror.

"Ever since you switched up the name and put that Cubana stamp on it, the business been booming. We got the whole city coming to the bayou to get our shit," Zoo said.

"Yeah, Tay is my good luck charm. Ever since I brought her here, we been running through them joints twice as fast. There's something about her," Saint said, not truly understanding how the business has nearly doubled since she's been in the bayou. It had been almost a year since she came back with him.

"Yeah, li'l sis got that voodoo shit on her," Zoo said jokingly.

Saint half-grinned and shook his head at Zoo's crazy explanation. "Nah, she just got a good vibe, bro. Took her from that bullshit, and the Trap God's blessing a nigga, ya hear me?" They burst out into laughter.

"Damn, Tay is legal now, huh?" Zoo said, thinking about how she was now on the market.

"Yeah, she legal, beloved," Saint answered.

"Can't lie, she a bad Cuban mu'fucka. Pretty as hell. That long hair and pretty eyes be having them boys going crazy. The young wolves around the way say she don't be giving niggas any play. Tell the truth . . . You hitting that?" Zoo asked, trying to get the real from Saint.

"On God, I have never touched her. I don't mess with young girls. I don't deal with no one. I'm serious about settling down with Mi," Saint said, giving him a serious look. "But check this out. I'm thinking about asking Mi to marry me tonight after Tay's birthday party," Saint said as he reached into the side center console and pulled out a small black box. He popped it open, and a shiny ring emerged. A huge diamond rock sat on a platinum band, and it sparkled brilliantly.

"Oh shit. You going to do it, huh?" Zoo asked as he examined the jewelry.

"Yeah, man. I think she's the one. She's been holding me down for so long and kept it G all the way through," Saint admitted.

"Yeah, Ramina is a real one, for sure. Plus, she let you bring a whole chick from Cuba and said nothing. Man, had that been one of my bitches and me, they would've been tried to cut me," Zoo said, only half-joking.

"Nah, Tay is like my little sister, man. That's my li'l baby," Saint said, meaning every word. They had established a little sister/big brother bond that was unlike any relationship that he ever had. Ramina had given her a job at her salon and accepted her with open arms after Saint broke down everything that happened to her. Tay's story broke Ramina's heart.

Ramina wasn't too happy at first, but once she met the girl and got to know her, Tay became like her protégé. Ramina had a love for Tay, and the little resentment that was there, in the beginning, was gone. They had agreed to let Tay stay in the upstairs loft above the salon, which Ramina had remodeled. So, it was more than comfortable. Tay would wash her clients' hair and sweep up the floor in return for money at the end of each week. The only stipulation was that she had to stay out of their way after hours when Zoo and Saint would count up in the back room of the shop.

Tay was slowly but surely getting her life together, and she owed it all to Saint. She adored him and looked at him as her savior. And that's precisely what he did. He saved her.

Chapter Twelve

Li'l Baby

Tay had a broom in hand sweeping up the floor as Ramina and her friends sat in the salon's chairs drinking wine. Music was lightly playing in the background. It was after hours in the shop. They were having a good time and partaking in girl talk, and, as usual, Tay didn't join in. She just listened, not being able to relate, so she remained quiet. She never had a real relationship, so the majority of their topics she couldn't add to. Ramina and her two best friends, Brittany and Vera, sat there talking away.

"And I swear I be so horny while I'm on my period. It never fails. Nigga look like chop liver when I'm off. Soon as my monthly comes—*Boom!* Nigga turns into Idris Elba," Brittany said as she gulped her wine. The girls laughed at Brittany's joke as they thought about their own situations.

"Betta tell that nigga to put a towel down," Vera added.

"Girl, I wish. He ain't 'bout that life," Brittany responded. They were having a good time, and Brittany felt sorry for Tay. She never joined in on their gossip, so she decided to open the floor to her.

"And what about you, Tay? I know yo' li'l ass be fuckin'," Brittany said as she waved her glass in her direction. Tay smiled and blushed. She giggled and shook her head in embarrassment.

"I know that smile from anywhere. You can tell us shit. We can be like yo' aunties. Gon', spill it. You ever gave one of these li'l niggas some pussy while you were bleeding? It be soooo good," Vera admitted. Brittany doubled over laughing and went over to Vera to high-five her.

"I don't have periods," Tay responded, embarrassed. It was obvious that she was ashamed and felt out of place. Ramina noticed her get uncomfortable and shot her friend a look that said, "That's enough, bitch."

"Hey, Tay, can you go upstairs and grab a bottle of wine for me? I left some in the cabinet," Ramina said, trying to break up the awkward tension.

"Sure," Tay said, giving a nervous smile.

Ramina watched her until she disappeared into the back. Once she saw that Tay exited the room, she shot a look at Brittany.

"Bitch, you talk too much. I told you she had it rough back in Cuba. The man she used to be with used to fight her like a damn dog. She was a full-blown athlete. You know athletes don't start getting their periods until they're twenty sometimes."

"Oh yeah. I heard that. Those female Olympians don't get their period until late too," Vera added.

"I'm so sorry," Brittany said as she put her hand on her chest, knowing that she was insensitive to Tay's early childhood abuse.

"On her damn birthday," Ramina said, adding fire to the flame. They had agreed to celebrate her birthday on the date that she arrived in America. On that day, it marked an entire year since she had been there.

"I ain't shit," Brittany playfully said as she downed the rest of her wine.

"You sure ain't shit," Vera said jokingly. Ramina smiled.

Then they heard Tay's footsteps as she returned to the room. They all ceased talking and tried to act normal.

Almost at the same time, Zoo and Saint walked through the front door. Saint had a birthday cake in his hand, and lit candles were on top of it. Ramina and the girls immediately started to sing "Happy Birthday" to Tay. It took Tay a second to figure out what was going on, but all the attention was on her, and she caught on quickly.

Happy Birthday to you,
Happy Birthday to you,
Happy Birthday to Tay,
Happy Birthday to you.

Tay was so surprised and happy to be celebrated. She put her hands over her mouth and was filled with joy. She couldn't remember the last time someone had done something for her birthday. She hadn't even realized that it had been a year already. She was just so happy to be free from Regis, she never thought twice about it. Saint walked right in front of her with the candle-filled cake. Tay closed her eyes and blew hard, blowing out all of the flames. A small cloud of smoke filled the air from the candles, and everyone clapped and crowded around her.

"Thank you so much, everyone. I appreciate this. I've never had anyone do something like this for me," Tay said as she enjoyed the moment.

"Let's get this party started," Brittany said as she turned up the music. They partied and had a good time all in honor of Tay. She was locked in as family.

It was approaching midnight, and Ramina hugged her friends as they headed out. Zoo had brought some tequila out, so they all were feeling good, including Saint. They even gave Tay a shot of liquor to celebrate her day. As the girls were leaving, Zoo leaned over to Saint and reminded him that they needed to count up before the night was over. He had the cash from all of their spots in his trunk and needed to make sure they were on point for the next re-up.

"But before we get into that, you gon' ask her?" Zoo asked, referring to the marriage proposal that Saint mentioned to him earlier.

"Nah, not tonight. I'm going to wait for a better time. Don't want to do it like this. I gotta put more thought into it for her," Saint explained.

"I feel that," Zoo whispered as they stood there conversing with each other.

Tay crept up behind them, coming from the bathroom. She hugged Saint from the back, slightly startling him. She hugged him so tightly, and her head was pressed tightly against his back. Saint smiled and patted her hand that was clasped snugly around his stomach. She slid around, and her tiny frame was tucked under his right arm.

"Thank you so much, big bro. This means a lot to me," she said while smiling. Zoo smiled and looked at her as well.

"No problem, Tay. That's what family does," he said, smiling as Ramina approached beaming. She felt good that Tay was in a good space.

"Yo, I'm going to the car and grab the bags," Zoo said. Saint nodded and watched him slip out the back. Ramina had a glass of wine in her hand and was noticeably tipsy. She slid under Saint's other arm. Now, he held them both and squeezed, giving them both a hug. He kissed Ramina on the lips and then pecked Tay on her forehead.

"I want to give you something," Ramina said as she moved from under Saint and grabbed Tay's hand.

Saint smiled as he watched Tay's eyes light up. They walked away, and Saint immediately looked at Ramina's huge backside.

"My big baby and my li'l baby," Saint said as he addressed them both. He would always play with Ramina and tell her she was a big baby because of how he had her spoiled. Ramina looked back and winked at Saint's comment. Saint smiled and watched them walk off into the corner to talk. He faded to the back so he could set up the money machine and begin the count up.

"I wanted to give you something," Ramina said as she looked down at Tay, who sat in the salon chair. Ramina reached into one of the drawers under the vanity mirror that lined the back wall and pulled out a book. It was a Bible.

"My grandmother gave me this when I turned 18 and told me that in life, whatever hurdles or demons I have, that I can find the remedy to them in here," Ramina said as she looked at Tay. A sticky note was on the front of it with Psalm 46:5 handwritten. "That was the first psalm she told me to look at."

Tay grabbed the book and hugged it tightly. It was the first gift she had ever gotten, and it meant a lot to her. Ramina wasn't heavy in religion at all, but she knew that Tay needed someone to do that for her. Her grandmother did it for her, so she would do the same for Tay. Ramina wasn't an angel, but she had a pure heart, and that was one of the reasons why Saint loved her so much. Tay got up and hugged Ramina and thanked her for the kind gesture.

"And tomorrow, I have us a spa day set up. Just me and you. No talkative-ass bitches tagging along," Ramina joked as they both shared a laugh.

Ramina grabbed the bottle of tequila off the counter and two red cups. "Okay, one shot for the birthday girl before I call it a night. I have to go home and get ready to put this pussy on Saint," Ramina said as she winked and stuck her tongue out of the side of her mouth.

"Aye," Tay said as Ramina did a halfhearted dance, moving her butt in circles. They took a shot together, and instantly, Tay felt it. After a few moments of small talk, Ramina called it a night and told Saint that she would meet him at home.

"All right, love, see you at home," Saint said as he sat at the table with no shirt on because the small room got hot. They would be there awhile. While he stuffed money into the top of the money machine, Ramina stuck her head inside the door of the back room and smiled. She told him that she was about to head out. She flicked her tongue at him in a freaky way, letting him know she wanted to taste him later. Saint knew that gesture well. They had been around each other long enough to talk without actually speaking. He knew that she was ready to get freaky that night. After the count up, he would head home to give her that masterful stroke, for sure. He smiled back, raised his eyebrows, and nodded his head, letting her know he was with it. She left, and he then focused on Tay. He watched as Tay walked past him and up the stairs that led to the upper loft.

"Good night, Tay," Saint said.

"'Night," Tay responded.

Zoo had on a wife beater as he paced the room and stretched his arms out. The table was full of money as the scattered bills almost covered the entire wooden table . . . so much that you couldn't even see the wood. Money was flowing in, and the Cuban dope was moving through the bayou like a plague.

"Yo, Li'l Cooda supposed to be hooking up some cable back here this week. We need to be watching SportsCenter while counting up this shit."

"Cooda? Li'l Cooda?" Saint asked, instantly knowing who he was talking about.

"Sharon's boy."

"Yeah . . . I remember Sharon. She died a few years back, right?"

"Right. She OD'd, remember?" Zoo reminded him.

"Yeah. Cooda is her son's name? That used to be my li'l partner," Saint said.

"Yessir. Li'l nigga out here bad on that shit, just like his mama," Zoo said as he shook his head.

"A shame . . ." Saint said as he stood up and watched the money flip through the machine.

Two hours later, they were at the end of the bag. The count was finally complete. They sat there and counted a little over two hundred thousand dollars, straight dope money. Saint sat back. The money felt good, but the smile on Tay's face felt better. That truly was the highlight of his night. As he rubber-banded the money, Zoo lit a blunt and wanted to run something by Saint.

"Yo, Tay was looking all right today. She a bad li'l one," Zoo said as he was feeling her style. "She reminds me of a baby Jhené Aiko," he said, referring to a famous singer as he took a deep pull of his weed.

"Oh yeah," Saint said as he handled the money. He shot a look at Zoo, and it was piercing.

"What's that, bro?" Zoo asked as he frowned and held his hands out, confused.

"What was what?" Saint said as he instantly knew what Zoo was referring to. He felt a type of way by Zoo's words, and he surprised even himself with his reaction. There was something that bothered him about Zoo addressing her like that, but he instantly shook that notion, knowing he was out of bounds.

"Nigga, I know you better than anybody. You soft on that girl," Zoo said with a huge smile.

“Nah, beloved. You off on that one,” Saint replied as he shook his head and focused on the last stack of money in front of him.

“Yeah, whatever, nigga. I know you,” Zoo said as he took the stacks off the table and stuffed them in the safe that was hidden behind a painting.

“You’re bugging,” Saint said as he smiled and took another shot of tequila.

“So, I’m about to head out. I got something on deck waiting at the room for me,” Zoo told him as he slid on his hoodie and the jacket. He closed the safe and then placed the picture over it, concealing it. Afterward, he slapped hands with Saint.

“Love you, bro,” Zoo said.

“Love you, beloved,” Saint said as he took another shot, thinking about Ramina’s phat ass and what he was going to do with it when he got home. He loved waking her up by way of his mouth, and he couldn’t wait to taste his woman. He watched as Zoo headed out the back, and then he heard the door slam. His cell phone buzzed, and he saw that it was a text from Ramina.

You still at the shop?

Yeah.

Zoo there with you?

He just left. I’m on my way home now.

Saint smiled at his text thread with Ramina, and the thought of sexing her made his dick begin to thump. He couldn’t wait to get home and get to her. He wanted to show her how much he had missed her. He stood up and slightly staggered. That’s when he knew he had had one too many drinks. *I gotta get home,* he thought to himself as he reached for his shirt and then his coat. Just as he was about to put them both on, he saw Tay come in.

“Hey, I thought you were asleep,” he said as he looked a bit surprised. She wore pajama pants and an oversized hoodie that she slept in.

"Oh . . . yeah. I heard the door close, and I was coming down to make sure it was locked before I went to bed," she answered.

"Cool. I'll make sure to lock up. Don't worry about it," Saint assured her.

"What you guys did for me today was really nice. I just wanted to say thank you again," Tay said as she walked over to him and hugged him. "Since I been here with you, I haven't touched any drugs and feel like a new person. I have you to thank for that," she said.

Saint wrapped his arms around her and kissed the top of her head. She hugged him so tightly, and he felt her brush up against his semi-erect penis. She slowly pulled back and looked up at him. Their eyes connected, and something urged Tay to kiss him. Saint kissed her back slowly, and she reached down to grab his rod and rub it. They continued kissing, and before you knew it, Tay was on her knees. Saint slightly stumbled, so he widened his stance to remain balanced. She pulled out his thickness and took him into her mouth.

"Wait . . . you can't . . ." Saint said, but it felt so good and warm. He threw his head back in pleasure and licked his lips, loving the warm sensation around his pipe. Tay slowly circled her tongue around his tool and bobbed on it. Saint felt kind of dizzy and then looked down at her, realizing what was happening. He instantly snapped out of it and regretted what he was letting happen. *What the fuck am I doing?* he thought to himself. Quickly, he looked over at the door, and his heart dropped. Ramina was standing there in her lingerie and a bottle of champagne with tears in her eyes.

"How could you!" she yelled as her heart broke into a million tiny pieces. He quickly stepped back and pushed Tay away as his hard dick popped out of her mouth.

"I'm so sorry," Tay said as she wiped her mouth and stood up.

"Baby, it's not what it looked like. I took too many shots and—" Saint tried to explain, but a flying champagne bottle came at him. It barely missed him as he leaned to the side. The bottle crashed against the back wall, causing shattered glass and champagne to spray everywhere.

"Fuck both of y'all. Y'all can have each other. What type of shit is this? After all we been through? Huh, Saint?" she screamed as her tears flowed. She then focused on Tay and tried to rush her, but Saint grabbed her as she lunged at Tay. Ramina kicked and screamed as she lost all control. She just saw red at that point. She was boiling.

"You dirty little whore. All I tried to do is help you. I want you to get yo' shit and get the fuck out of my shop. Get the fuck out now!" Ramina shouted as she pointed at the door. "If I see you around here again, I'll fucking kill you! Leave!"

Tay cried profusely, hyperventilating. She couldn't even respond. She just kept apologizing, but none of that mattered to Ramina. "Get out!" she yelled again, feeling that Tay wasn't moving fast enough.

Tay rushed to the door and out of the shop. She ran down the block to get away from the madness and didn't know what to do or where to go. She leaned against the wall of a building and slowly slid onto her bottom. She buried her head in her lap and cried like a baby. "What did I do?" she asked aloud as the tears streamed down.

"Are you okay?" a young man riding a bike said to her as he headed in the direction of the shop. He stopped right in front of her and placed one of his dirty shoes on the sidewalk pavement to balance himself. Tay looked up and saw the gap-toothed young boy. She hadn't seen him before.

"Hey, it's okay. It's okay. What happened?" the boy asked. "Are you hurt?" he said out of concern, thinking she had been raped or something like that.

"I just fucked up my life . . ." Tay said as she looked past the young boy, not focusing on anything in particular. She was talking to herself more so than to him.

"What's your name? I'm Cooda."

Chapter Thirteen

Three Months Later . . .

A furry brown rat ran across the wooden floor, but it didn't bother Tay. Although she hated rodents and was terrified of them, it didn't seem to matter. She focused on the task in front of her. The trash-littered home was filled with drug paraphernalia and empty bottles that had been used and tossed aside without a care. A rusty gun sat on the table as well. The owner of the house left it there, and Cooda toted it everywhere since the day that he discovered it.

The vintage couches were soiled and stained from years of careless use. The carpet matched its griminess, and the walls were covered in outdated wallpaper. The stench of body odor filled the spot. It looked as if a hurricane had blown through the living room. Tay and Cooda had been in this abandoned house that Cooda had illegally connected electricity to. He had stolen it from the next-door neighbor. The abandoned house acted as their crash house for the past few weeks. Cooda was on the couch with one thing on his mind, and that was getting high. A belt was wrapped tightly around his right arm as he rested his elbow on his knee.

Tay impatiently waited as she pulled the belt tight, trying to help Cooda find a suitable vein. She carefully watched as he smacked his arm repeatedly, attempting to make a vein bulge. As he eyed his arm, he saw a fat, greenish vein form and knew he was ready to indulge. His mouth watered, and an orgasmic feeling approached. The pure anticipation of the drug made him high without it even being in his system.

"Pull a little tighter. Shit . . . Come on now, Tay," he begged as he smacked his arm one more time. "Yeah, there it go," he said as his vein was to his liking. It looked like a fat gummy worm lying under his skin. It was the perfect candidate for injection.

He reached over and grabbed the syringe that was on the table and slowly pushed out the water that danced on top of the heroin. He carefully injected the needle into his bulging vein and slowly emptied the syringe. When he pushed all the dope into his vein, he pulled the needle out and placed it on the table. Then he sluggishly leaned back on the couch and closed his eyes. He smiled as he felt the warm sensation creep up his arm. He slowly grabbed his crotch area and squeezed as the drug worked its magic.

He opened one eye and watched as Tay hurriedly set herself up for her hit. She held a lighter under the spoon and waved it slowly, wanting to distribute the fire equally. She watched closely as the heroin liquefied. Then she grabbed the syringe and sucked up all the dope. The anticipation was killing her, and sweat beads formed on her nose as she anxiously prepped for her trip to cloud nine.

She reached over and unwrapped the belt from around Cooda's arm. She placed it on hers, prepping for her turn. She tightened the belt, placing it in between her teeth. As she clenched down, her jawbone flexed. Slobber dripped out of the side of her mouth as she anxiously searched for a good spot to poke. She jerked her head back violently, making it even snugger. She waited until a big vein formed and grabbed the needle with her free hand. Then she cautiously slid the needle in and let it flow.

"Ooh. Oooh shit," she crooned as she slowly slumped on the couch. Her body relaxed. To her, it felt like she were melting. It felt so good. She was shoulder to shoulder with Cooda, and they were experiencing forbidden heaven together. The drug felt so good as it traveled into her bloodstream and worked its undeniable magic.

This had become an everyday thing for the pair. Ever since the big fight with Ramina, Tay had been in the streets with Cooda. She didn't have anywhere else to go, so the streets were her only option. Cooda had pulled her into the downward spiral of being a junkie.

"This feels soooo good," Tay said as she closed her eyes and smiled.

"This that good shit," Cooda responded.

"Uh-huh," she hummed in agreement.

"They loved you on the strip. We gotta go back," Cooda said as he referred to the downtown area that was known as the ho stroll. After Cooda begged her, she eventually gave in and agreed to turn a few tricks. She told him that she would only give head, though . . . That was her stipulation. Somehow, that made her feel better about what she was doing. From the johns, they got a lot of nos, but the yeses they did get were enough to make a few bucks. She earned enough for them to score the drugs and stay high all day.

As Tay slipped in and out of her nod, she thought of Saint and how things had panned out. She lost track of time since the last time seeing him. She missed him so much and didn't know how much she depended on him until he wasn't there. The big blowup that caused her to leave was too much to recover from. She wished that drunken night had never happened. There was so much about herself that Saint didn't know, and she felt guilty that she never would be able to tell him. As she nodded, water formed in the corner of her eyes. As the warm tears ran down her cheeks, she slowly drifted into a drug-infused sleep . . . thinking about the good times.

Zoo and Saint sat in the back of the shop, counting up the money from the month. It was their ghetto ritual that they did every first Sunday, a day that the shop was closed as well. Zoo, as usual, picked up all the money from around the bayou and brought it back to the shop. They had been there for a few hours, and it was now approaching three a.m.

"It's getting late as hell," Zoo said as he pulled on the marijuana-filled joint and slowly blew it out. Saint quickly waved the smoke away from his face as it drifted over to him.

"My bad, brody," Zoo said, not meaning to send the smoke in his direction. Saint had just wrapped a rubber band around the stack and placed it neatly in the bag that was below him.

"That's a half right there," he confirmed as he zipped up the bag. He was referring to the half a million dollars that he would be taking to Alexandro.

"Bet. When are you headed back?" Zoo asked.

"Next week. We are going to Dubai for a weekend, and I'm going to leave from there," Saint explained.

"Damn, bro. Y'all stay taking trips. Must be nice," Zoo teased as he counted the money. The joint dangled from the left side of his mouth.

"The trips aren't for me. They're for her. That's the key," Saint explained.

"The key?" Zoo asked.

"Absolutely, beloved," Saint said as he stood up and stretched. He then continued. "The key to keeping a woman happy is making sure she has something to look forward to. That's all a woman really wants. She wants something to get dressed up for and look forward to."

"Damn . . . That's deep. Maybe that's why I can't keep one," Zoo said as he paused his counting and nodded in approval.

"Might have a point," Saint responded.

"Yo . . . speaking of, peep this shit," Zoo said as he jumped up and went over to the TV screen that was on the corner of the wall. "So last week, I installed cameras in the shop. A few nights ago, I had shorty come through, and she brought her friend." Zoo pushed a button on the DVR, and an image popped on the screen. It was Zoo having a threesome right in the middle of the main floor of the barbershop. One thick, chocolate woman was riding his face, while another slim girl was bouncing on his shaft. The moans and slurping noises sounded through the speaker as they were caught on the hidden cameras.

"Peep how she working that ass," Zoo said in excitement as he smiled and pointed at the screen. He bounced his hand along with the girl's ass that was riding him. "*Bam . . . bam . . . bam,*" he said playfully as they both watched the peep show.

"You crazy than a mu'fucka, beloved," Saint joked as he shook his head and looked away. He grabbed his jacket and then picked up the duffle bag from the floor. "I got to get out of here. Hold it down while I'm gone. Remember to put seven thousand in the bank each night at the nightly deposit box," Saint said, reminding him of their strategy to wash their money.

"Go and enjoy yourself. I'll take care of everything here," Zoo assured him as he walked over and slapped hands with Saint.

"In a minute," Saint said as he always did. He walked out and headed home to his woman.

***

"He's just different," Ramina admitted as she sat on the couch with her legs tucked under her butt. The girls sat in Saint's home right in the middle of the living room. An oversized bearskin rug was their pallet, and the lights were dimmed. They all crowded in front of the fireplace as the flickering fire illuminated the room. The smooth sounds of Summer Walker's ballads provided the soundtrack for their girls' night in. Vera and Brittany accompanied Ramina, sharing wine and laughter, having a great time. The midnight oil burned, filling the room with the sweet almond aroma. They had been there for the past three hours laughing, talking shit, and getting tipsy. Ramina was trying to explain the difference between Saint and her past lovers.

"OK, bitch, you have to explain. What's so different? Spill the beans," Vera stated as she downed the last of her Merlot and wiggled in her chair, excited about the tale ready to be revealed.

"I know, girl, tell it," Brittany said as she clapped her hands, egging her friend to go on with the steamy details.

"Okay . . . okay," Ramina said as she blushed. She put her hand on her face, hiding it. Her cheekbones became apple red, and her light brown skin exposed her discomfiture. "Pour me another drink, first," she said as she stretched out her glass and waited for Brittany to give her a refill. As Ramina watched her wine getting poured, she spoke.

"It's different. It's hard to explain but . . . It's like a massage," Ramina said as she closed her eyes, getting flashbacks of her encounters with her man. She felt a tingle in her love button and crossed her legs to feel the friction.

"A massage? Y'all be on that tantric kick?" Brittany asked. She was well invested in the details.

"No, not like a massage with his hands. He massages me with his dick," Ramina said as she smiled widely. "Okay, so . . . he has this thing he does . . ." she said, just before pausing. Her girls were attentive and oozing off her every word. Ramina continued as she closed her eyes to reflect.

"So, this nigga rubs your body with his dick. Like with baby oil and all?" Vera said, trying to understand what Ramina was getting at.

"No, girl. Listen, it's like he massages my insides. He slowly goes in deep. I mean deep . . . deep. Then he just slowly rocks and goes in small circles. Whew, child," Ramina said as she placed her hand on her chest and took a sip of her wine.

"Okay, Saint massaging the coochie, huh? I heard that," Brittany said while laughing.

"These other men need to take notes. Especially the young ones," Vera exclaimed.

"Girl, yes. These young niggas be trying to beat my shit up. I mean, damn. I be sore for the entire next day."

"Y'all are too crazy," Ramina said, not being able to relate. They all burst into laughter, having a good time enjoying girl talk. All the sex talk had Ramina thinking about her man. She looked at her phone and noticed that he had texted her.

Be home in an hour, love.

Ramina's mind instantly drifted to him stroking her, which made her squirm in anticipation. She decided that she should do something special for him before their trip to Dubai. She had put him on pussy punishment for the past three months because of the incident with Tay. She felt betrayed. However, Saint had been a good sport about it and didn't complain once. They had been on four trips since it happened, and she could tell that he was really remorseful. So, at that moment, she decided that she would put it on him good that night. She texted back, deciding to cook something up special for him when he came home.

Dinner will be on the table . . .

Ramina took the bottle and downed the remaining wine. She wiped her mouth and looked at her girls. "It's time for y'all to go. My man is on his way," she said as she headed toward the stairs. "Y'all can let yourselves out," she said, while not even turning back around to look at them. She only had an hour to prepare Saint's special meal.

Chapter Fourteen

Medusa's Snake

The midnight chill was swirling in the air, and the hawk was out. It was an unusually cold night for the bayou, but that didn't stop the streetwalkers from going up and down the block selling sex. Men with short shorts, heavy makeup, and bad wigs roamed the small back street. Their muscular builds and wide shoulders made it clear what their true gender was.

Most of the streetlights had been shot out, so the full moon acted as the only illumination. On this particular back street was a small community of society's outcasts and the freaks who sought them. It was an area that was taboo, and the district was looked down upon by the locals. This was the part of New Orleans people never spoke of, which is why Tay stuck out like a sore thumb there. This wasn't her world; yet, she had to do what she had to do. After no luck on the main strip where the ladies turned tricks, Cooda suggested they visit there to try their hand with the freaks. At first, Tay was against it, but the insatiable pull of the drug and her desire to feel it in her veins overruled all. She wasn't the boss of her life anymore. . . the dope was. Cooda convinced her, saying, "A freak is a freak. At the end of the day, they want their dick wet. Let's just try it." Tay eventually gave in, and there they were . . . trying to feed their addiction on the backstreet.

Cooda stood against the brick wall and watched Tay closely. He observed intensely in hopes that she could get the customer. They desperately needed money, and Cooda had no other ideas. He was even open to trading his body and services for a score. That night, it seemed like the tricks weren't looking for what he was offering, so Tay was their only hope. They had been chasing for the past few hours since they had awoken from their heroin-induced nod from earlier that day. Cooda knew that time was ticking before the stomach pains would kick in from withdrawal. At that point, they were just desperate. He stared at Tay, feeling like he was standing on pins and needles. She was leaned over into the passenger-side window, and the bottom of her small cheeks hung from the bottom of her short skirt. A black Lincoln pulled to the curb, and a middle-aged white man was behind the steering wheel. Cooda shifted his weight from his left foot to his right as he frantically scratched himself on his arms.

"What is he saying?" Cooda whispered harshly, trying to figure out what was going on. Tay looked back at Cooda in irritation and quickly held up her finger, signaling for him to hold tight. As she turned her head toward the car, the sound of tires screeching erupted. The abrupt sound startled Tay, making her jump back. The car peeled off while leaving a cloud of smoke. Tay stormed back toward Cooda, rubbing her hands together and blowing on them, trying to stay warm.

"Damn, Cooda, you scared him away," she said while shaking her head in disappointment.

"Sorry, Tay," he said, knowing that he messed up.

"It's okay. He didn't want what I had anyway," Tay said, not wanting to be too down on her only friend. She saw him sulking and tried to crack a joke to lighten the mood.

"He wanted one of the linebacker dudes walking down there . . . not me," she said as she looked down the block at the two muscular men that stood on the corner. They both got a good laugh out of it and cackled together.

"Let's get out of the cold for a second. I still have some change in my purse. We can get some hot chocolate from McDonald's until we figure out our next move. Standing out here ain't going to get us nowhere," she admitted.

"OK, cool, because I'm freezing my balls off," Cooda joked as he shook his shoulders playfully.

"Mines too," Tay added jokingly, which sent them into a fit of laughter. Cooda loved how funny Tay was, and he adored her. He never had a friend like her before. She was the only person in his life who didn't judge him for who he was. She understood him, and he loved her for it. Seeing her laugh brightened up his day.

"I love you, BFF," Cooda said as he threw his arm around Tay's small shoulders.

"I love you too, best friend," she replied, and with that, they headed around the corner to the restaurant to game plan how to get the monkey off.

"Aye, didn't you say they used to count money in the back of the shop on Sundays?" Cooda asked.

Saint grabbed the duffle bag from his trunk and slammed the door shut. He took a deep breath and patted his stomach. He had been so busy that he hadn't eaten all day, so the text that Ramina had sent him about dinner was just what he needed. He entered his home and saw that the light was dim, and he could smell oil burning. He also heard music lightly playing from upstairs. He automatically assumed that Ramina had company over earlier. He was used to the burning oil on their girls' night, so the smell was very familiar to him. He opened the closet by the front door and set the duffle bag in before making his way toward the kitchen.

"Mi, I'm home, love," he yelled upstairs to let her know he had arrived. As he made his way to the kitchen, he pulled off his jacket. He wanted to get comfortable so that he could eat dinner and get some much-needed rest. They had an early flight, and he hated traveling groggy. As he pulled his shirt over his head, he steadily walked toward the kitchen. He yelled loudly for Ramina again. "Love, what you cook?" He thought she could hear him from downstairs.

As he reached the kitchen with his shirt off, he saw a beautiful presentation. Ramina wore a full-bodied fishnet suit with red stilettos on. As she sat on the edge of the table, her legs were propped up, giving him a clear viewpoint of her glazed lips. Her freshly shaven vagina was on full display, and it was a sight to behold. Her bright red lipstick matched her shoe color exactly, and she was au naturel under the net. Her thick body filled out the suit. In fact, it seemed as if she would burst out of it at any moment.

"Come get your dinner," she seductively said as she put two fingers in her mouth to wet them. She ran her tongue around her fingers and pulled them out, letting spit sloppily drip from them. Next, she took those same two fingers and let them fall to her love box. She seductively spanked her clitoris, making a loud, wet sound resonate throughout the house.

Smack!

Smack!

Smack!

The sound of her hand smacking against her skin instantly aroused Saint, and he gripped his member through his jeans, slowly stroking it for preparation. Ramina kept direct eye contact with him, never looking away. The faint sounds of music by DVSN played in the background, and the mood was set.

She softly caressed her erect button, applying light pressure to it, then moaned while slowly moving her hips in circles. She was slow winding the lower half of her body like a snake, and her movement was in perfect unison with her two twirling fingers. As she masturbated, Saint stood there in awe, watching the erotic show in front of him.

"Damn, baby," he said in amazement as his eyes were fixated on her plump vagina. It started to drip onto the marble tabletop. She spread her legs a tad bit wider, exposing her pinkness. Saint felt his member harden to its fullest potential. It had been so long since he made love to his woman, and he was patient. He understood that he had been wrong, so he didn't want to rush the healing process by forcing sex on a broken heart. But from what he was seeing, he knew that it had been worth the wait. His tool was as hard as a missile. He slowly walked over to his woman, who was steadily playing with herself. He dropped down to his knees, and just so happened, his face lined up perfectly with her love below. He could smell the sweet musk coming from his woman, and it turned him on even more.

He moved Ramina's hand away from her love box and replaced it with his mouth. He carefully French kissed her clitoris, gently sucking it while unhurriedly flicking his tongue from left to right, then up and down. He knew how she liked it, so he was extra soft and tender as he kissed it. He took his time, looking at it and making sure he was perfectly lined up before he went back in. He put both of his hands on her inner thighs and used his two thumbs to open her lips for better access.

He pulled his head back and admired her hard button sticking out. He kissed it repeatedly and carefully worked on her with slow, wet pecks making a loud, smooching noise every time he did it. It was getting good to Ramina, so she grabbed the back of his bald head and plunged his head into her box with every peck. She stretched her neck, looking down so that she could see the magic happening. She noticed that her juices got caught in his beard, dripping off of it and onto the floor. The visuals drove her crazy, and she coached him.

"Suck it harder, baby," she whispered as she squirmed and continued to bob his head, but this time with force. She gradually slammed his face harder and harder into her wetness, causing a splashing noise with each slam. She stared intensely, and a crazed look formed on her face as she was in a trance of pure pleasure. Seeing his face, white teeth, and gold row turned her on to the fullest. She was in complete bliss and opened her mouth, panting heavily. Her eyes slowly rolled in the back of her head, and her body got stiff. She momentarily made an ugly and confused face as she groaned. She felt all of her tension building up, and the lack of sex had her anxiety built up to the max.

She continued to crash his head into her love box. It seemed as if she were trying to stick his whole head inside of her. Her feet went into the air, and her moaning became screams as she felt a huge orgasm approaching. One of her eyes involuntarily closed, and she felt her toes curl. Saint moaned, feeling it was getting good to her, and that sound alone sent him over the top.

"I love you! Oh God . . . I love you. Shit, boy," she yelled as her body shook. That's when liquid shot out of her and splashed against Saint's face like a tsunami. She squirted all over his face and chest as her body quivered uncontrollably. Saint wiped off his face and dropped his pants, showing his rock-hard member. He smoothly slid inside of her as he placed his thumb directly on her clitoris. Taking his tool, he went as deeply inside of her as possible and then slowly applied pressure to her button with his thumb. He expertly worked his thumb in circular motions. With his free hand, he lifted one of her legs and ran his hand down it, until he reached her heel. He popped off her shoe so that her bare foot was in his hand and close to his face. He slowly brought her foot to his mouth, skillfully licking her toes. He did this while still rubbing her button, keeping the pressure intact. He gradually worked his hips, moving his hard rod subtlety inside of her.

They made love that night all over the house, and it was long overdue on both of their behalves. They desperately needed to catch and release, and that's exactly what they did. The two reconnected that night, and what Saint had done with Tay was just an afterthought not worth a mention.

Just before the sun came up, Saint had gotten calls back to back to back. He finally got around to answering them, knowing it had to be urgent. It was Gunner, telling him that Zoo had been shot and robbed. Saint got up and rushed out of the house, heading to the hospital. He had to get to the bottom of what had happened.

Chapter Fifteen

Deceitful Intentions

Zoo watched Saint closely as he stood next to him. They were in the back of the shop. Saint kept rewinding the tape and pausing it on certain parts that displayed the shooter's tattooed arms. They were in the back room of the store, watching the playback of the recent robbery. Zoo had studied the tape for what seemed to be a hundred times before he had called Saint to notify him. Saint shook his head, not believing Tay's audacity. Zoo had on an arm sling and was bandaged on his shoulder. He had gone to the hospital and got looked at after the robbery. Luckily, the bullet went in and out, not hitting anything vital.

"I helped her in so many ways, and look, beloved," Saint said. He seemed as if he were in a daze. "*This* how she repays me, huh? I brought her over here from Cuba to have a better life, and she does *this* bullshit?" Saint said, talking more to himself than Zoo. Zoo had never seen Saint so angry. It was out of his character. Not until that very moment did he understand the hold Tay had on Saint.

He watched closely as the robbery went down. They had Zoo on the floor at gunpoint. Saint's heart was broken into pieces knowing that Tay would stoop that low and commit the ultimate betrayal. He watched as the scene played out, and Zoo ultimately ended up getting shot.

"That's Li'l Cooda from the block. Li'l sweet nigga," Zoo said, pointing him out on the screen monitor. Tay had on a ski mask, but her tattoos and petite build were a dead giveaway.

"The li'l dude that be hooking up the cable?" Saint asked to confirm.

"Yeah, that's him. Had a weak, rusty-ass gun. That's prolly the only reason I'm still here," Zoo replied.

"How much did they get?" Saint asked.

"The whole week's take."

Saint calculated in his mind and knew that it was over 200k. That wasn't little enough to let slide.

"Fuck!" he yelled as he put his hands on his belt buckle and slowly paced the room.

"I know where he be at, though. The wolves already got the drop on him for me. They're in an old bando on the East Side," Zoo explained.

"Say no more. Call the wolves off. I'm going," Saint said with fire in his eyes.

Cooda and Tay were lying on the soiled couch, both in the middle of a nod. They had just shot five hundred dollars' worth of heroin into their veins over the past forty-eight hours. They robbed Zoo, and this was the fruit of their labor. They coped some dope away from Saint and Zoo's territory and spent the past two days getting high as the moon. They didn't even notice the new visitors. Saint crept through the unlocked front door along with Zoo. He quietly walked up on the two sleeping beauties with a chrome .45 in his hands. The drug-induced duo slowly bobbed up and down, repeatedly jerking their heads up when their chins touched their chests. They made this same motion for the past hour. Saint looked on the floor and saw a familiar duffle bag, which confirmed what he didn't want to believe. He pressed the cold steel of his gun to Cooda's forehead, making him jump up.

"Wake up, youngin'. Let me talk to you," Saint said calmly. Cooda took a good look at him and stared for a second. He then closed his eyes and tried to go back into his nod. However, Saint gently tapped his temple with the gun. "Wake up," he said this time with more bass in his voice. This made Cooda jump up and look around again. He looked at Zoo and then at Saint, knowing what time it was.

"Hey, man. What's going on?" Cooda asked as he sat upright and backed away as far as he could, almost crawling up the couch to get away from the barrel of the pistol.

"You robbed me?" Saint asked calmly as he smoothly crossed his arms in front of him, letting the pistol dangle by his crotch area.

"Nah . . . You got the wrong one, man. I would never do that," Cooda said as he started to shake like a leaf.

"What's that by your feet?" Saint asked as he looked over at the bag. Cooda's eyes followed Saint's, and he trembled even harder. Tears formed in his eyes as he tried to gather himself to speak. Saint bent down and grabbed the bag. He tossed it to Zoo, who was standing by the door. Zoo caught it with his one good arm and placed it on the floor. Then he immediately opened it up and saw that not too much was missing.

"Most of it's here," Zoo said calmly.

"How much you shoot up?" Saint asked as he put his gun in his waist. Cooda instantly cried, knowing that he had fucked up.

"I'm sorry, man. This shit got a hold of me, man. I'm so sorry." Cooda pleaded as he buried his face in his open hands. The sobbing made Tay wake up, and she quickly realized the situation and froze with fear.

"Again, how much of my money did you shoot up?" Saint asked with more aggression in his voice this time.

"About two hundred today and three hundred yesterday," Cooda admitted.

"So, you traded your life for five hundred dollars' worth of dope," Saint said as he couldn't wrap his mind around their audacity. He quickly pulled out his gun, and Cooda tried to put his hands up to block the bullet, but Saint was too fast. He shot two bullets in Cooda's dome, sending him flying back onto the couch with double wounds to his skull. Tay screamed and panicked as the brain splatter from Cooda's head was all over his face. Blood was everywhere as Cooda's eyes were open, and he stared into space as blood oozed from the bullet holes.

"They say if you die with your eyes opened, you deserved it . . ." Zoo said as he stepped forward. He leaned over and whispered to Saint, "Want me to take care of her?" he asked, knowing that would be a harder task for Saint.

"Nah, I'ma let her live," Saint said as he stared at her with clenched jaws. He pointed his gun at her head as she held her hands up and hyperventilated. "I want you to leave this city. If I ever see you again. I'm going to do you just like I did your friend. You hear me?" Saint said boldly with no emotion. Tay nodded swiftly with her hands still held up.

"Now, get the fuck outta here," Saint as he stepped to the side and watched her leave with a heavy heart and guilty conscious. Their bond would forever be broken.

Epilogue

Present Day

Ramina cried as she slipped the packet of bad dope into the Bible. She had it from when it fell from Saint's pocket the night before. She went back and forth about putting it in the book. However, her rage was as deep as the ocean, and she knew that this would be the only way to even the odds. For some reason, Tay had a hold on her man.

Matthew 27:3–4, that's what she wrote on the sticky note. She placed the bad dope on the same page as the verse, so Tay would find it and hopefully put it to use. Ramina was tired—tired of loving a man that never picked her. Even when she gave him a second chance, he didn't choose her. All she wanted was Saint to love her, and that was something that he refused to do. What was supposed to be the best day of her life, which was her wedding day . . . turned out to be one that she wished never happened. She placed a note on their bed, hoping Saint would find it. She requested that he urged Tay to read the verse that she quoted "for her own good."

"Lord, forgive me," she whispered as she stood up and left the room. Before she left, she peeked into the guest room and saw her man sleeping, sitting bedside of Tay. With that . . . she quietly left.

Ramina cried a cascade of tears as she sped down the highway, pushing nearly eighty miles per hour. The top was dropped as she glided in and out of lanes on the interstate. She needed to feel the force of the wind. She wanted to *feel* it. She had to feel something . . . something other than what she was feeling on that early morning. Everything was just so heavy on her soul, heavier than anything had ever been. Her entire being was shaken, and everything that she knew was for certain somehow was now unreliable. The picture-perfect life that she finally thought she had seemed to be snatched from under her. The only man that she truly loved was in love with someone else. She could tell. She just knew. There was something about seeing those tears in Saint's eyes that told her the truth. Not his words or his actions, but those tears told her everything that she *didn't* want to know. She had been with him for years and never once saw tears from that man.

Ramina had no makeup on her face, and her natural brown skin glowed in the sunlight. Being in public like this was a rarity for her. She hadn't walked out of the house in years without being dolled up. But on this day, she just had to get away from the anguish that was back home.

She slightly raised her oversized sunglasses with her index finger and wiped tears away as she wept. She cried uncontrollably as she thought about how her husband was at home tending to that dope-sick woman, rather than celebrating their new marriage with her. The loud purr from her silver Porsche Panamera ripped through the airwaves. She neared one hundred miles per hour. The sounds of Lauryn Hill knocked through her sound system as her long, jet-black hair blew wildly in the air.

She was supposed to be on an airplane on her way to Italy for her honeymoon. Instead, she was in still in the bayou . . . heartbroken. She was there wondering if she had made a mistake by marrying Saint. *How can he be trying to put her together, while I'm fucking falling apart?* she thought as the tears continued to flow. She had loved Saint with every morsel in her body, and she knew he was a good man. The problem was that he was being a good man to someone else. Anxiety crept in. Although she tried to breathe slowly, the heartache was overweighing it all.

"Why does he love her? I fucking hate her! I *hate* that bitch. I wish she would just die," Ramina cried as she smashed the accelerator to the floor, pushing the luxury vehicle to the limit. She was now nearing one hundred twenty miles per hour. Somehow, the speed seemed to help her release the unwanted tension that had built up inside of her.

Ramina's disappointment and frustration had reached its boiling point. She felt like she was being robbed—robbed of the life that she had deserved. She stood by Saint's side and played her position the right way throughout the years. The pain slowly started to become rage. She possessed a massive flame that burned deep within her soul, all behind the man that the streets feared, and the ladies lusted after. She was drawn to his quiet power. She was addicted to him, and she wasn't going to let him go.

"Fuck that!" she yelled as she squeezed the steering wheel as tightly as her grips would allow. She let out a roar of passion that she never knew she had.

"Aaaagh!" she screamed, which turned into a gut-wrenching sob. She angrily hit her steering wheel. She wasn't a hateful person, but over that man, she would become the worst. He was her trigger. *He was her trigger.*

She felt something in the pit of her stomach rumble as nausea set in. Suddenly, the urge to throw up overwhelmed her. She was sweating profusely and dry heaving while becoming dizzy. Vomit came up in her mouth. She leaned over to spit the vomit out in her passenger seat. Her eyes grew as big as golf balls when she saw all the clear secretions that she had thrown up. But it wasn't the spit and secretions that alerted her. It was the small green frog hopping around in it, struggling to escape the thick liquid . . .

What the fuck? she thought as she tried to refocus her fuzzy vision. Her heart raced rapidly. She was confused and frightened at the same time. She shook her head and focused on the road . . . but it was too late.

The sound of a thunderous crash resonated in the air, followed by screeching tires and crushing metal. Ramina crashed her car into the back of an eighteen-wheeler semitruck, instantly propelling her body into the air like a rag doll. She was launched about fifty yards and crashed violently onto the pavement. Her body rolled over a dozen times against the concrete, ripping her flesh with each flip. It all happened so fast . . . She never saw it coming.

Saint received an urgent call from the paramedics saying that Ramina had been in a bad car accident. Without hesitation, he dropped everything and stormed out. He left Tay at his home alone without hesitation. Guilt lay on his heart, and he knew that he had neglected the love of his life, Ramina, for another woman. Mixed emotions were running through his mind as he worried immensely. His white Range Rover sped at over 100 miles per hour en route to New Orleans East Hospital. He made it a point for Ramina to keep his name in her emergency contacts, inside her wallet. So, they prepared for something like this. However, he never imagined it would happen.

"Please, God, make sure my baby is okay. Please . . . please, God," he pleaded as he gripped his steering wheel so tightly that it hurt his hands. After a fifteen-minute high-speed drive, he violently pulled into the hospital and hopped out. He didn't care about anything or anyone at that point. He left his car running and door open as he ran full speed into the emergency room. He approached the emergency desk desperately, asking for help. He still had on his same pants and dress shirt from his wedding the previous night.

"Ramina Scott . . . I mean Ramina Cole. I need to know where Ramina Cole is. She's my wife," he said as his heart beat rapidly, and worry was heavy in his eyes. A short, pudgy African American woman sat at the front desk while typing on a computer. She ran her finger down a list and stopped at a name. She read aloud.

"Psalm 34:18," she said. Well, that was what Saint heard.

"Excuse me?" he asked, not understanding what she meant by that.

"I said room 3418, sir," the lady said, looking at Saint as if he were crazy. Saint rushed toward the ICU where Ramina was, hoping like hell that she was okay. As he reached the room, something came over him. His body froze before his hand touched the doorknob, not knowing what would be on the other side.

As he opened the door, he saw Ramina lying on the bed with tubes coming out of her nose and mouth. The sight alone made his knees buckle, and he instantly started to cry. He cried a river, and his eyes were glued on the love of his life. She didn't even look like herself. To see her that way was agonizing.

"No . . . No, baby," he whispered while breaking down. He stood over her and gently rubbed her head. His hand shook so badly that he couldn't even properly comfort her. He snatched his hand back and covered his mouth to stop his involuntary cries from seeing her swollen mouth, eyes, and lips. Her two front teeth were knocked out, and her head looked twice as large as it regularly did. He had never felt this weak in his life. He felt powerless that there was nothing he could do to help her. He wondered, *What happened? How? Who hit her? Who or what did she hit? Is she going to be OK?* There were so many things going on in his mind, and he couldn't understand what she did to deserve that. She was the purest soul that he had ever met. Little did he know, Karma seemed to have visited her.

Tay sat there and looked at the pack of dope that sat on the Bible page. Her high had come down, but that gigantic monkey was still climbing her back. She needed to get it off in the worst way. Her skin crawled, and the pains inside of her stomach were close to unbearable. She was living through hell, literally. She stared at the dope pack as tears welled up in her eyes. She wanted to flush it down the toilet, but her urge wouldn't let her do it. She couldn't understand why Ramina would have left something for her like this. *Maybe she didn't want me to fight the pains of withdrawal,* she thought to try to justify her self-destructing habit. She let that be the reason and grabbed her jacket, frantically looking for her shooter and lighter. Once she found them, she raced downstairs, rushing to the kitchen. She grabbed a spoon from the kitchen drawer and headed to the bathroom. Then she closed the door behind her and sat on the floor as she put her works together. She grabbed one of Saint's belts that hung on the back of the door and quickly wrapped it around her upper arm and made sure it was tight. She repeatedly smacked her arm with two fingers, causing a nice vein to form. She melted the drug down and liquefied it. Tears rolled as she filled her syringe with the poison.

Tay reflected on everything in her life and how difficult it had played out. She thought about how her parents disowned her, forcing her to the streets to prostitute herself. She thought about Regis picking her up and making her fight and sex his friends like she was a dog. She thought about how she crossed the line with Saint. She betrayed him in so many ways that he would never know. She thought about finally finding someone who understood her pain and secrets as Cooda did. He knew exactly how she felt and related to her on so many levels. Then she thought about how her actions got him killed. Thinking about all of those things . . . made her fill the needle. She slowly injected the heroin into her vein.

She smiled and noticed rain fall outside of the window and thumbed the windowpane. Lightning flashed in the sky, making her smile. Any other day, it would have looked like bad weather, but at that moment, it seemed so pretty, so beautiful. It seemed as if God were snapping pictures of the rain. Tay smiled as her eyes slowly rolled to the back of her head. Suddenly, her body started jerking violently. Foam bubbled out of her mouth as she slid onto her back . . .

Tears filled Saint's eyes as he walked into the room where the coroner waited. Saint walked over to him and took a deep breath and blew it out slowly. He was there to identify the body. His heart was broken into pieces, and he wished that he could turn back the hands of time and make things so much different from what they were. The elderly white man put his hand on the sheet and peeled it back. Saint looked down and saw Tay's purplish face as she lay there naked on the cold steel. He took a deep breath and gave the coroner a quick nod to confirm. Next, the coroner pulled the sheet back, so it exposed her entire body. Saint's eyes drifted down, and his heart dropped when he saw a small penis on Tay.

His knees got weak, and he almost fainted, wondering what the fuck was going on. His whole world was turned upside down. He was confused. However, the truth was there all the time. He just never noticed. Neither did you . . .

The End

A teaser . . . for what's to come!

The Streets Have No Queen

by

JaQuavis Coleman

This isn't a sequel, but a well thought out puzzle.
Everything connects. It always does . . .

—JaQuavis Coleman

Prologue

A man lay comfortably on a brown leather couch, intensely staring at the ceiling. He had little to no movement as his eyes fixated on a small imperfection on the surface. His head was slightly propped up by a small pillow. The room was quiet . . . well, almost. Nothing but the constant sound of the steel balls clinking as they swung back and forth on the pendulum filled the air. Most people called this Newton's cradle. It caused a constant ticking echo throughout the dim room. A brown hue from the desk lamp hovered over the office, and the faint smell of vanilla danced around. Hundreds of books lined the bookshelves against the walls. A woman sat off in a corner with a notepad in hand, studying the man on the couch. She watched his every move.

"At first . . ." the man said in a low tone just before pausing. He took a deep breath, cleared his throat, and clenched his jaw firmly. He was trying his hardest to fight off tears and took a hard swallow. He inhaled deeply and slowly exhaled, almost as if he could release some of the pain he had built up in his chest by merely blowing it out. He closed his eyes and spoke. "At first, she asked if we could jump with no plan. I said, 'Fuck it, I'm with it.' I was all in," the man said, choosing his words wisely as they came out.

"They say love is exactly like skydiving. If you really think about it, that's some real shit. Love is a fucking free fall. You truly don't have any control of the outcome once you've committed to love someone. Shit's crazy, right? Just think about it. You don't 'walk in love,' and you don't 'run in love.' You fucking '*fall* in love' . . . that's what her love was like. It always felt like I was falling. No control. No foundation. I was just falling. It was the greatest feeling in the world to me." As he lay there, a single tear slipped down his face, traveling down to the rim of his ear. The man quickly sat up and shook his head in grief.

"Bless, please continue," the doctor said as she gently tapped her pen on her notebook. The beautiful Dr. Celeste Ose was a Haitian-born psychiatrist. She had perfect ebony skin and high cheekbones. Her natural kinky hair was pulled neatly into a bun on top of her head. She was slightly intrigued by Bless. He was so mysterious, and he was a man she couldn't quite understand. She repeated herself eagerly, wanting him to resume.

"Please . . . continue," Doctor Ose said. Again, he said nothing. She had been seeing him for months, and he had never talked about *her* for more than a sentence. She saw progress, and she wanted him to keep going to enable her to dig deeper. Doctor Ose paused and waited for a response. He remained quiet and seemed as if he were in deep thought, searching for the right thing to say.

"I can't. I just see red when I think about her. All I can see is red," Bless said as he shook his head in grief.

"I know it's upsetting and hurtful to lose a spouse, but the first step to healing is to—" The doctor said, but before she could finish her sentence, the man stood up and grabbed his blazer.

"I'm sorry, Doc, I have to go," he said as he gave her a forced grin. "I appreciate your time."

"I understand. I'll see you next week for our next session, correct?" Doctor Ose asked as she smiled back with understanding eyes.

"Yeah, sure. I'll be back," Bless said in a low tone just before exiting the office, leaving her sitting there puzzled. In all her years, she had never had a patient so complicated and so hard for her to get a breakthrough. Doctor Ose reached over to her desktop and stopped Newton's cradle. She contemplated referring him to a different doctor to see if someone else could help him, but she chose to keep trying.

Bless had been coming to the doctor for six months straight, and their sessions never went more than ten minutes because of his unwillingness to talk about his deceased wife. He would start and then just abruptly leave. Every. Single. Time. However, on that day, he spoke longer than he ever had before, and because of that, she knew he was making progress. Doctor Ose's professional integrity wanted to refer him elsewhere, but her greed stopped her. You see, Bless was a high-profile client. He paid in cash every week and always paid triple the invoice. His only request was that his files would be kept secret, and he came after hours. It was evident that he was a very private patient. She didn't know exactly what Bless did for a living, but by the way he paid . . . she knew he did it very well.

Bless got into the back seat of his luxury Maybach and instructed his driver to go to the cemetery. He wanted to talk to Queen, his deceased wife. He needed a release. He needed to speak to his best friend to try to find some sort of clarity. On that day, her death weighed heavily on his spirit, and he felt himself breaking down. Bless knew that death was a part of life, but the way she left him was something that he couldn't accept. He watched aimlessly out of his window as they maneuvered through the Detroit traffic. Although cars, nature, and pedestrians were in his eyeshot, the only thing he could see was the face of the love of his life. Her smile is what he missed the most. The way her dimples were deep always made him smile. Queen had dimples so deep that you could securely place nickels in them. Her chubby cheeks and her sweet smell was something that he would never forget.

Scattered pictures of Queen flashed in his mind, causing him to smile from ear to ear and randomly chuckle when he thought about the way she laughed. Her laugh could make any room a happy one.

The twenty-minute ride only seemed like a minute or two because of his extended daydream. As the vehicle entered the cemetery, the pain slowly crept back into Bless's chest. He grabbed a small briefcase from the next seat and exited the car. The closer he got to her grave, the more Bless could feel his wife's presence. It was a bittersweet feeling because he could always feel his heart get heavier with each step when he made his way to his baby. The harsh reality that she was buried six feet underground plagued his thoughts.

Bless finally approached where she rested and took a deep breath. He looked at the three-foot tombstone and examined the wording. It read, *My Earth. My Isis. My Queen. Fall 1990–Rise 2018.* The cemetery staff and tomb makers pleaded with Bless when they got the tombstone wording request. They tried to convince him that he had it backward. Every time, Bless would laugh and simply answer, "If you knew her . . . you would know it's 100 percent correct." He and his wife would always talk about how loving each other was like falling, and he laughed at their inside joke that the world didn't seem to get. Leaves covered the cemetery lawn since it was the middle of autumn. The trees were almost bare, and the light wind made small, beautiful tornados in various parts of the walkway.

Bless approached the grave and rubbed his hand over her name. “My Queen . . . my Queen,” he whispered as his eyes teared up. He had married his dream girl and found the love of his life. Not too many people live without regrets, but up until her death, Bless had none. He was happy, content, and free when he was with her. Queen understood him, and he got her. They had been childhood classmates, and as they grew, so did their love. By high school, they had already vowed to each other that they would spend the rest of their lives together. The word *soul mate* didn’t do their union any justice. Their bond was spiritual. Their bond was unbreakable. Their bond was no more. Bless pulled off his jacket and laid it on the grass. He sat down and opened his briefcase.

“Hey, pretty girl. I had a rough day today. Wanna hear about it?” he whispered as he wiped a tear away. He dug into the bag and pulled out a small blank canvas and a few paintbrushes. He started his routine as he prepared to do a small painting while talking to her. This was something that they did while she was alive, and it brought him peace then, and it seemed to do the same thing now.

An hour passed as Bless painted a picture while casually talking to his wife as if she were sitting there with him. He laughed, cried, and reminisced, all while re-creating the cemetery scenery. The speckled orange and red leaves were scattered throughout the canvas with so much detail that you could see the veins within the leaves. Bless even added a small fox in the background to complement the esthetics of his creation. He smiled, knowing that Queen loved the way he always strategically did things and painted with precision. She would tell him he was like a mad scientist with his paintbrush. She had always been his number one fan.

Bless continued to paint until the sun set and then headed back to the car to go home. It was a rough day for him. His days were up and down, and this particular day was a down one. He just wanted to go home and sleep the pain away. Sometimes, you have to sleep and give your pain to God, and that's what his plans were for that evening.

The driver returned Bless to his home, and he immediately poured himself a glass of Cognac and put on some jazz. The smooth and soothing sounds played throughout the house, and Bless started to unwind. He loosened his shirt and kicked off his shoes as he went to the back window that overlooked a pond. The moonlight bounced off the water, and he stood there, admiring the scene. Bless took a small sip of the aged Cognac and closed his eyes as he savored the taste and the excellent music. He heard thunder, and shortly after, the rain came down. He smiled, remembering how Queen liked to make love when it rained. For some reason, the sound of water crashing against the ground made her love flow. The spacious home always seemed cold to him after Queen left. It never really seemed like home without her being there with him.

The smooth sounds of trumpets soothed his soul. Bless swayed back and forth, enjoying the moment . . . until an unexpected bell chimed. He instantly shot his eyes toward his door. *Who is that?* he thought to himself. He never had guests, so he wasn't expecting anyone.

Bless was confused as he set his drink down and made his way to the front door. He opened the door, and to his surprise, a stranger was standing on his doorstep. It was a young lady that looked to be no older than 25. The rain was pouring down, and she was completely soaked. He looked into the woman's face in confusion, wondering if she was at the wrong house because he had never seen her a day in his life. She had kind, big brown welcoming eyes, and her hair was soaked and stringy. It hung past her shoulders. The young lady had a bundle in her arms and what sounded like a screaming baby. She had it wrapped loosely in a pink blanket. She rocked her baby as she whispered to it, trying to keep it calm. She tried her best to cover the baby's face from the rain as she rocked it, trying to keep it quiet. The loud crying was as if the baby was in pain and immediately tugged at Bless's heart. A child was something that Queen always wanted, so he thought of her instantly.

"Hello, sir, so sorry to bother you, but my car broke down just up the road. My phone is dead, and I didn't know what to do," she said as tears filled her eyes.

"Sure. Sure. Come in, sweetheart," Bless said as he instantly wanted to help. His heart couldn't let him leave a crying baby and distressed woman outside in the thunder and rain. He looked at her frame and noticed that she had a similar build to his Queen and immediately thought about grabbing an old hoodie for her. "Let me grab my phone for you. Also, my wife was about your size. Let me see if I can find you some dry clothes."

"Bless your heart. God is good. Thank you so much," the woman said, as she continued to rock the baby, trying her best to keep it calm. However, the crying just got louder and more frantic. "I'm sorry. She's terrified," the woman said as she looked down at the baby and whispered to it again. Bless turned around to head to his coffee table where his phone was.

"It's okay. You can use my phone to call who you need while—" Bless said as he headed to the next room, but he stopped midsentence when an iron bar crashed against the back of his head. Bless fell forward and lost consciousness before he even hit the ground. He was out cold. A man with a bright skin tone and multiple scars on his face stood above him. He had snuck in right behind the woman when Bless turned his back.

"Let's get it," the man said, as he looked back at the woman whose face was once innocent, but now had a sinister look on it. She dropped the blanket that was in her hand, letting her "bundle of joy" drop on the ground. The sinister woman smiled as she carelessly dropped the small speaker box that she had wrapped up. The recording of the baby crying sounded through the speaker box even louder now that it was exposed.

"Turn that bullshit off. Grab the ropes from outside. Let's get this nigga tied up before he wakes up," the man said as he dropped the crowbar and scanned the house.

"I'm on it, daddy," the woman said as she quickly did as she was told. Bless had let the devil in, and that's when the game began.

Chapter One

Bless woke up groggily and in a compromising position. He was sitting upright in a chair, and his hands were bound by rope, tied behind his back. He realized that he was in his own living room and tried to make sense of what had got him there. The last thing Bless remembered was answering the door and nothing much after that. The back of his head throbbed, and when he saw the unfamiliar man standing in front of him, he looked in confusion.

The fair-skinned intruder was light bright and seemed to be the next step above albino. His eyes had red circles around them, and his lips were so pink that it looked as if he had a touch of lipstick on them. This was an unusual-looking man. He had a weathered face. Scars were all over his cheeks and forehead as if he came directly out of a comic book. He definitely looked like a villain—the evilest type.

"What's going on? Why am I tied up?" Bless asked with a shaking voice. Fear was obviously present inside of him. It was all in his demeanor and tone.

"Rise and shine, sweetheart," the man said sarcastically. He circled Bless and scrutinized him. He smiled and noticed that Bless was just as his partner described him . . . a four-eyed, soft-spoken man. An easy target, to say the least.

"I think you might have made a mistake," Bless pleaded.

"No, we have the right house. Believe that," the man said as he looked around the house and admire the paintings on the wall.

Bless looked confused as he sat there. While being bound to a chair, Bless looked around and tried to get a grasp on who was in his home. He looked at the young lady who had been at his front door, asking for help. She was now sitting on his counter, eating a bag potato chips, as if she didn't have a care in the world. The man stopped directly in front of Bless and looked down on him.

"I'm not even going to play with you, my nigga. We know what's going on, and you do too. This is a stickup. We came for the paper," Red said with confidence as he rubbed both of his hands together. He had a stern look in his eyes, and Bless stared directly into them. Bless felt like he was looking at the devil directly in the face. The man didn't blink once, and he had a look of not giving a fuck. Bless instantly knew that the man didn't have it all and was legit crazy. It was written all over his face.

"A stickup? Paper?" Bless asked while frowning up. The man grew enraged and was not in the mood to play games. He gave Bless a swift and powerful punch to his midsection. Bless folded over like a lawn chair as he let out a grunt from the thunderous blow.

"Okay, let's try this thing again," the man said as he aggressively placed his hand on the back of Bless's neck and pulled him slightly. He kneeled so they could be face-to-face. The man wanted Bless to look directly into his eyes and see that he wasn't with any type of game. He wanted to be firm and clear in his intentions. "I'm going to be blunt with you," the man said as he intensely gazed at Bless. Without breaking eye contact with Bless, the man reached out his hand and wiggled his fingers, signaling his woman to hand him the gun.

The woman hopped off the counter and grabbed the gun from the countertop. She quickly walked it over to her man and placed it in his hand. The man, in a single sweeping motion, placed the pistol directly against Bless's forehead. The cold steel against his skin made Bless realize that it was a real situation.

"Okay . . . I get it. Please don't hurt me," Bless conceded.

"Now, we're getting somewhere," the man responded while smiling. He stood up, but not before pushing Bless's head forcefully, causing him to jerk back violently. "I know that you have that delivery this evening, and I need that bag. Understand me?" Red instructed. Bless instantly dropped his head in defeat, knowing that he had gotten caught slipping.

"Damn, man," Bless whispered to himself as he shook his head in disbelief. He had moved so cautiously and low-key. He had dotted all his i's and crossed his t's. How did this happen?

"I know, right? It's kinda fucked-up, playboy," the man said playfully as he slowly circled Bless. "You opened your door to a woman in distress and a crying baby and got much more. Life is fucked-up, man. Tell me about it. I know more than anyone how cold this world can be. But dig this . . . I don't even want to kill you, my nigga. I just need that paper," the man said.

"It's not coming tonight," Bless admitted as he avoided eye contact with Red.

"What the fuck did you just say?" the man quizzed as he grabbed the back of Bless's neck again.

"I said, it's not coming tonight. My mule got stuck in Denver on a layover. He won't be here until tomorrow night," Bless admitted.

"Don't fucking play with me!" the man yelled as frustration set in.

"I'm telling the truth. He texted me about an hour ago, letting me know that his plane was delayed. Check my phone and verify it. It's right in the messages. My phone is in my pocket," Bless suggested as he looked in the direction of his right pocket.

The man immediately grabbed for Bless's pocket to retrieve the phone. He pulled it out and read through the message threads. The most recent message was one from Watson. The man instantly clicked on the name. He knew the name because of the intel he got on his mark. Watson was the moneyman and was the person who delivered the cash to Bless. He read the message, and it confirmed what Bless had alleged. Watson had informed him that he would be over the following night when his new flight landed in Detroit.

"Fuck!" the man yelled in frustration as reality set in.

"What, baby?" the woman said as she hopped off the counter and walked over to her man, whose eyes were still fixated on the message. The man showed her the text on the phone, and her joy was also taken.

"Well, what are we going to do, Red?" she asked, panicking.

"Bitch, what did you just say?" Red harshly whispered as he used his free hand to wrap around her neck. The woman put her hands up, conceding, as she gasped for air. Red was squeezing her throat so hard that it blocked her airway, and veins formed on her temples and forehead. He lifted her, causing her to stand on her tiptoes as he looked at her with disgust. "You said my name, you birdbrain bitch."

"I'm sorry . . . I'm sorry," she managed to whisper, knowing that she had slipped up and made a big mistake by saying his name. Red slightly eased up on his grasp, then released her, letting her fall to the ground. She held her neck and violently coughed as she tried to catch her breath.

"Dumb ass," he said as he shook his head in disbelief while looking down at her beneath him. Bless just looked on, feeling sorry for the woman. Then Red refocused his attention back on Bless.

"Well, it looks like we're going to be here for a while. Ain't that right, *Shawna?*" Red said, making sure her name was yelled out in the open as well. He didn't care either way at that point because he had already decided to kill Bless after they got the money.

Red knelt and rubbed Shawna's hair away from her face, exposing her wet cheeks. "Sorry, baby," he whispered in her ear as he cradled the back of her neck and awkwardly kissed her. "You just have to be smarter, OK?" Red instructed. Shawna nodded her head in agreement as her tears still flowed, causing her mascara to streak down her face.

"Well, sir, I guess we're going to have a little sleepover. Time to get comfortable," Red said with a demented facial expression. He was going to wait until the money got there, and then he would murder Bless. Red's mind was set.

Chapter Two

A man in his late 20s sat patiently in a mint-conditioned vehicle. He looked around in awe, admiring his surroundings. He gripped the woodgrain circle that was in front of him and tightened his grip on the mint leather. He slowly cracked a smile as he stared at the world-renowned symbol that rested square in the middle of the steering wheel. He couldn't believe that he was in the driver's seat of a Bentley—the same car that he used to dream about having while staring at a cutout of it on a cement wall. Just three months earlier, he was sitting in a federal penitentiary in the Upper Peninsula of Michigan. He shook his head in disbelief as he checked his rearview mirror. He saw the sign that read, *Arrivals*, as he sat curbside at Detroit Metropolitan Airport.

"One day . . . one day," the man said to himself under his breath as he imagined whipping the vehicle through his old neighborhood. He slowly traced the outer steering wheel with his right hand. He was determined that soon he would enjoy it as an owner rather than his current position as a chauffeur.

Luck had been on his side, getting a great job through a work-release program. Initially, Fonz wanted to return to the street game so that he could get back on his feet, but instead, Fonz felt this job was a blessing sent from above to steer him in the right direction. He vowed to fly straight for as long as he could, and this route seemed to be the best option. Also, he loved the position's perks. It wasn't bad for an alternative to a life of crime. The job was simple. Every other Sunday, he picked up his boss and took him to the airport. Then twelve hours later, he picked him up to return him home. The best part of the job was that it paid in cash, which was helpful because between Fonz's three kids and their two mothers, child support drained any check that came through his pipeline, not to mention an ill mother that he cared for.

Fonz was working the current gig along with a third-shift job as a security guard. It didn't pay much, but he was doing the best he could with the opportunities placed in front of him. It was a far cry from his past life, and he had switched his lifestyle tremendously since he'd been out. No matter how hard Fonz tried to convince himself that he could get used to living below the poverty line, he knew that it wouldn't last long. He was accustomed to having money since his early teenage years, and his current situation wasn't cutting it for him. Fonz needed more.

Alfonzo Coolidge was the name of the driver, but in the streets, he went by the moniker, Fonz. He was an ex-convict who had a reputation for robbery. He was pretty good at it too. As far as he was concerned, he would have never gotten caught if it wasn't for him taking on a partner who eventually snitched on him, landing him in front of a judge. He spent six years in jail for a simple in-and-out job at a local check-cashing joint. Fonz vowed never to go back.

Fonz checked his wristwatch and then over to his right. He focused on the double doors, looking for his client to emerge from the airport. Just like clockwork, his client came walking out of the building.

A tall, lean, dark man with a cell phone to his ear headed toward the car. He looked to be in his mid- to late thirties and had a shiny bald head. The man wore a well-tailored charcoal suit, looking as if he stepped off the pages of the latest *GQ* magazine. His perfectly straight white teeth sparkled as he moved his mouth while talking on the phone. They seemed even brighter against his deep chocolate complexion. The man wore reading glasses, and his posture didn't match his appearance. He walked with a sense of insecurity and seemed to be an introverted soul, avoiding eye contact with people as he maneuvered through the sea of travelers. The man walked with a certain bashfulness that screamed "insecure." He carried a leather briefcase and swiftly made his way over to the car after spotting it at the curb.

Fonz noticed Mr. Brigante awkwardly weaving through the crowd and making his way over to the car. He quickly checked his mirror to glance at himself and straightened his tie. He pulled up his collar, trying to hide his big neck tattoo that read "*Linwood,*" paying homage to his neighborhood in the inner city of Detroit. Fonz quickly exited the car and went to the passenger side, reaching for the handle. He opened the rear door, timing it perfectly with his boss's stride.

Mr. Brigante ducked his head and slid in smoothly, never breaking stride or even acknowledging Fonz. Fonz closed the door behind him and made his way back into the driver's seat. Not wanting to interrupt his boss's conversation, Fonz nodded to greet him. Mr. Brigante casually waved his hand as he continued his business call. Fonz strapped on his seat belt and merged into the lane heading out of the airport.

Fonz listened carefully as he always did when the man discussed his business, hoping he could learn something by eavesdropping. Fonz always wondered what the hell his boss was involved in. He knew that it was something illegal, just because the boss always dealt in cash and moved with a certain mystique. He didn't peg him as a drug dealer. He was much too timid for that. However, he did get the referral from a known drug dealer, and he knew that birds of a feather usually flocked together.

Maybe he sells black market organs or funds illegal heists. What type of time is this nigga on? Fonz thought to himself as he merged onto the freeway.

For months, Fonz always wondered what line of work his boss was in but never had the balls to spark up a conversation to dig deeper. The one thing Fonz knew for certain was that it was something that he wanted to keep from the government, which, nine times out of ten, was always an illegal endeavor. No one knew much about his boss.

"These art units were beautiful. Not one flaw in them. They will sell quickly for sure. The flakes in the picture looked like fish scales," Mr. Brigante said to the other person on the phone. Fonz listened and smirked slightly, knowing that Mr. Brigante was speaking in code. Fonz was much too slick for that disguised lingo to go over his head. To the untrained ear, one would think Mr. Brigante was talking about a painting. However, the way Fonz heard it, he was describing a batch of drugs coming in. Hence, the code word "units." Also, Fonz heard him say there were "no flaws," which wasn't referring to actual flaws. He was referring to the units being pure and unstepped on.

Who this nigga think I am? An amateur? I can decipher homie whole convo, he thought to himself while continuing to listen.

"Great, so once it's done, text me the final number. Good job, Watson. See you tomorrow evening," Mr. Brigante said just before he ended the phone call and focused on Fonz. "It's Alfonzo, right?"

"Uh, yes, Mr. Brigante," Fonz said, not expecting his boss to talk to him.

"Mr. Brigante is my father. Call me Bless," he said as he smiled and loosened his tie.

"Bless?" Fonz asked, making sure he heard it right.

"Yeah, I know . . . It's uncommon, right? My mom had a vivid imagination. She always said there's power in one's name, so she decided to name me Bless," he said, cracking a small smile.

"Well, sir, if you don't mind me saying . . . She was telling the truth. You are definitely blessed," Fonz said as he rubbed the dashboard in appreciation. Bless chuckled lightly.

"You can say that, I guess. Moms always know best," Bless said as he unbuttoned his cuff links, getting more comfortable. Bless stared at Fonz for a second and then said, "What about your mom? Is she still living?" he asked.

"Yeah, she's a trooper. She's battling cancer and taking it day by day," Fonz replied.

"Sorry to hear that. Do you see her a lot?" Bless questioned.

"I work two jobs, and I try to get over there to take care of her as much as I can. The plan is to save up enough to eventually get her a nurse a few times out of the week. Ya know, to help her out a bit while I'm away," Fonz said.

"I lost someone special to me not too long ago. It's tough. You should spend as much time as you can with her because time is the only thing you can't get back. It's the most valuable thing on this earth," Bless said as he looked forward as if he were staring into space, not particularly looking at anything.

Fonz nodded in agreement but didn't respond. He appreciated the advice knowing that Bless was telling the truth. Fonz wanted to keep the conversation going because his employer had never said more than two words to him during the three months that he had worked for him. He wanted to figure out what exactly Bless did for a living. The mystery was killing him, and since the ice was broken, he thought that was his way in.

"So, what line of work are you in?" Fonz asked as he checked his mirror and switched lanes.

"I'm a painter and an art dealer," Bless responded.

"Business must be good," Fonz said as he cracked a smile involuntarily.

"It's booming," Bless said with a smirk. He looked at Fonz, and they made eye contact through the rearview mirror. Fonz knew at that moment that Bless was into some illegal shit. Fonz had doubts before, but he knew a criminal grin when he saw one. He nodded, knowing nothing more needed to be said.

"Turn that up for me, please," Bless said as the faint sounds of jazz pumped through the speakers.

Fonz quickly dialed up the music and continued to cruise down Interstate 75, heading to the quiet, secluded suburbs of Auburn Hills. Fonz remained silent the rest of the way to Bless's residence. However, his mind unremittingly started to churn. He had been raised in the streets, and the prize position is either a plug or a wealthy target. Either way, Fonz wanted to learn more.

Half an hour later, the luxury car was pulling into the long driveway that led to the extravagant home. Just as usual, a modest Honda Accord was sitting there parked. It was Fonz's mom's car and what he was using to get around until he got on his feet. He always parked his car there and switched vehicles before coming to pick up Bless.

When Fonz parked, he quickly hopped out and skipped over to the back passenger side to open the door for Bless. Bless stepped out and nodded to Fonz before picking up his ringing cell phone. Fonz closed the door behind him with his mind running a thousand miles per minute. He wanted to take advantage of the opportunity to build with Bless, so he went for it.

"Excuse me," Fonz said, as he held up one finger trying to catch Bless's attention.

Bless, still engaged in his phone conversation, turned slightly, and looked at Fonz to see what he wanted.

"Sorry to bother you, but may I use the restroom?" Fonz requested, trying to gain access to Bless's home as an attempt to get in good with him. Bless paused as if he was thinking hard about it and then nodded in agreement.

"Sure, I guess. Come on in," Bless said as he headed to the door.

Fonz quickly closed the door and followed Bless up the walkway. Fonz didn't show it physically, but he was beaming on the inside. He could spot people like Bless from a mile away. The brains behind an operation, but he had no street in him. In a world of sharks, Bless was something that you called *food*. Fonz could tell Bless didn't have any toughness. It was all in his demeanor. Bless lacked self-confidence, which usually meant a man was weak.

Fonz admired the property's immaculate landscaping as he followed close behind. He observed as Bless approach the door. Rather than pull out a set of house keys, Bless placed a thumb on a sensor and held it there for a second. Then the sounds of a few deadbolts clicking erupted. Bless ended his phone conversation and pushed the big steel door open. Fonz was amazed at the technology. It was something that he had never before witnessed. The sophisticated entry method blew his mind, and Fonz watched as he stepped over the threshold, entering the home. Marble floors lined the house, and a gush of cool air hit Fonz's face as he trailed behind. The smell of lavender filled his nostrils. Bless stepped to the side to give Fonz a pathway to walk.

"The bathroom is down the hall and to the right," Bless said, as he looked at Fonz skeptically.

"Thanks," Fonz responded as he walked down the long corridor and admired the remarkable paintings that lined the wall. The abundance of radiant colors and abstract objects were stunning to the naked eye. The lights had a trickle effect, so each step he took, the area of the hall would light up. Fonz looked around in disbelief as the seemingly futuristic home amazed him. Then he spotted the bathroom to the right and stepped in.

Bless took off his suit jacket and got settled in his home. He walked into his marble kitchen and placed his briefcase on top of the counter. He then rested his hands over the sink and took a deep breath. He looked over at the life-sized, hand-painted portrait of his wife and smiled, admiring her beauty. The smile instantly turned into grief as he closed his eyes, remembering the only true love of his life.

Queen sat naked in the chair. Her shoulders were pulled back, and her posture was immaculate. Her body glowed radiantly as her smooth, cocoa complexion was on full display. Her big, long legs were crossed, and her extra serving of loveliness was hanging over the sides of the stool. Queen wasn't a small lady by any means, but she was well put together. Her plump, smooth baby skin was moisturized with natural oils, and it was as if she were shining. Her sides had small rolls where her ribs were, and her wide hips were on full display. She slowly bopped her foot to the smooth music as Badu played in the background.

The smell of sage burned throughout the home, mixed with the scent of marijuana. Queen subtly took a pull of the joint as she bopped her head to the music. Her breasts were perky, sitting high, and her full, dark areolas were on exhibit. Her natural hair was wrapped in a multicolored head wrap, and only the soft baby hairs that rested on the edge of her scalp were visible. Queen smiled as she caught the eyes of her man studying her intensely.

Bless's piercing stare contained extreme passion and admiration as he crossed his arms, squinting his eyes. He was covered in paint and was shirtless with snug-fitting khakis. Different specks of paint were all over his body from his hours of creating, using different shades, trying desperately to re-create Queen's honey-brown complexion. He stood barefoot in the middle of his garage with his paintbrush in his hand. He was painting what he considered one of his most important pieces ever.

"I'm almost finished, my love. Thanks for being patient with me," he said in a low, baritone voice.

"Patience is mandatory when you're in love with a man. What would I ever rush anything for? We have an entire lifetime to experience together. Patience is—"

"A virtue . . ." Bless cut in, finishing her sentence as he stood before her, examining her facial features. Bless froze as he looked into her big brown eyes, and the urge to cry overcame him. His soul was connected to hers. There was no mistaking that. He understood that love like hers came once in a lifetime, and that, alone, gave him tears of joy every time he thought about it. She was gentle. She was kind. She was patient. Most importantly, she was his woman. They had been together since they were teenagers. Queen put the marijuana-filled joint to her lips, taking a deep pull of smoke into her lungs. Then she slowly puckered her lips and blew out a stream of creamy smoke. The smoke drifted into Bless's face as he squinted and smoothly turned his head.

"I'm sorry, daddy," Queen said while smirking at his cuteness. She rubbed the side of his face and giggled. She frequently blew trees to relax and get her in a familiar vibe. However, she felt guilty, knowing that Bless wasn't a smoker. "I'm going to stop smoking one day," she said. She watched as he turned back to her with a small grin.

"No worries. Do what makes you happy, love. Everyone has an addiction. Mine just happens to be you." Bless stated it with sincerity while he stared at her in admiration. He leaned in and kissed her deep right dimple, then her left dimple, and followed it with a gentle kiss to her forehead. Bless held the kiss on her forehead and whispered, "My pretty girl." That move of his always sent sparks through her spine. It never failed. While most men thought that women had a cord connecting their clitoris to their heart, the real "hot spot" was their foreheads. That's where women truly felt love at. For that is the spot where women usually experience their first kisses.

A parent usually shows their love for an infant by kissing them on their forehead. It is subconsciously embedded in a woman's anatomy to feel real love by this type of kiss. Only a man that paid attention to detail understood this. Queen closed her eyes and swayed back and forth as if music were playing. There was no music playing, but their vibration was real and on the same accord. She could feel it moving her.

"I love you," she whispered.

"I love you too, pretty girl," he responded, as he stepped back and went directly to his large canvas mounted on the wall. He swiftly stroked his paintbrush and continued crafting his chocolate Mona Lisa.

Fonz exited the bathroom and headed down the corridor to the kitchen area where Bless was. The hallway walls were full of paintings, and splashes of red were throughout each one. Fonz looked closely and admired the works of art. The attention to detail was stellar, and thick cedar oak wood frames outlined all of them. The high ceilings in the house seemed to make his footsteps echo even louder throughout the quiet home. The technology blew his mind as Fonz, once again, looked down at the floors as they lit up with each new step.

He studied each painting as he went past them and noticed a recurring theme in each one. They all had a fox as the main focal point. Fonz even saw a painting that had a man posing in a suit; however, his head was that of a fox. Every painting was different with the fox being the common denominator. Surprisingly, the fox made it all come together. The color clashes and intricate pallets were visually stunning. *This looks amazing!* Fonz thought as he looked on in admiration. He reached the kitchen and saw that Bless had taken off his shirt and only wore a beater. He was already engaged in painting when Fonz walked in.

"Uh . . . Thanks for letting me use your restroom, sir," Fonz said, as he walked up on him. Bless was so locked in on his painting that he didn't even look back at Fonz. Fonz stood there awkwardly and waited to see if Bless was going to acknowledge him, but he didn't. Bless was beginning to paint on the canvas that was propped on the wall. "I'll just let myself out," Fonz said unsurely.

"Sorry about that. I didn't want to lose this vision I had for my new piece," Bless said as he used his index finger to balance his glasses on the bridge of his nose. He then set down the paintbrush and wiped his hands on a towel that laid nearby. "You want a beer?" Bless hesitantly asked as he walked over to the refrigerator and opened the door.

"Hell yeah," Fonz said. He couldn't control his eagerness, and the words just slipped out of his mouth.

"Great." Bless pulled out two longneck bottles. "Here ya go," Bless said. He tossed one over, and Fonz quickly caught it. Bless popped open the bottle and began making his way over to where Fonz was standing.

"Cheers," Bless said, as he raised his bottle and pointed at Fonz. Fonz then popped his open and followed suit, clinking his bottle's neck with Bless's.

Clink!

Both men took a swallow, and Fonz nodded his head in approval at the taste. "This is some good stuff," Fonz said, as he examined the foreign-looking bottle.

"Yeah, it's Irish beer. I get it shipped directly to me. Only kind of beer I drink," Bless said, smiling as he took another swallow. "You play chess?" Bless asked as he threw his head in the direction of the table that was off in the corner.

"Chess? Hell yeah, I can play a little," Fonz said, as he nodded his head. Fonz's gamble had worked, and he had gotten Bless to open up a bit. Fonz knew that he was one step closer to see exactly what type of business Bless was in. He knew that selling those paintings had not gotten him the house and the lifestyle that he was living. Fonz was determined to find out Bless's game. He didn't know exactly how, but he did know one thing: he wanted in.

"This is a nice-ass house, bruh. The floors, the lights . . . Everything is so futuristic. Some real fly shit," Fonz said, as he sat at the table and looked around.

"Thanks. I love new technology. I have the most modern systems installed throughout the house," Bless answered.

They sat down and played. Fonz carefully watched the man across from him, trying to figure him out. Bless's timid nature and the way his shoulders would always hunch over were a dead giveaway of his meekness. As they played, Fonz noticed that Bless would occasionally check his phone as if he were waiting for something. Fonz tried to eye hustle and see what was on his screen, but he couldn't get a good look from where he was sitting across the table. Bless studied the board strategically and remained quiet as he made his moves against Fonz. It was obvious that Bless was much more advanced than Fonz, as he quickly removed his pieces on the board, knocking them off one by one.

"I'm kind of rusty. Haven't played since I been home from Upstate," Fonz shamefully said as he moved his queen piece across the board.

"I can see that," Bless said calmly as he looked at his phone again. A text had just come through. He slightly grinned, then set his phone down. He refocused on the board and then looked up at Fonz. Bless used his index finger to prop his glasses up on the bridge of his nose and smiled nervously. "Check," he said.

"Damn," Fonz said as he studied the board, seeing that he had no way out. He was trapped. He knew the game was about to be over.

"See? You play fast and without a plan. Chess is a thinking man's game," Bless stated.

"You got me. You got me," Fonz admitted as he pretended like he cared. However, inside his mind, chess was the last thing he was thinking of. He didn't give a fuck about the game they were playing. He just was trying to make a connection, so if losing a few chess games helped Fonz do that, he was all for it.

"You're not so bad. You just rush. I can see it all in your game. I was baiting you with every step," Bless said in a matter-of-fact tone.

"Baiting?" Fonz asked, trying to understand what Bless was talking about.

"Yeah, bait. One of the laws of power is 'use bait, if necessary.' This works well in chess too. I did it on you all game," Bless said, breaking down his tactics for Fonz to understand clearly.

Bless's phone buzzed, and he glanced at it and nodded his head in approval.

"Checkmate," Bless said, as he took down Fonz's king. He then looked at Fonz, smiled, and took the last swallow of his beer. "Give me a sec. I have to take a leak," Bless said as he stood up and hurried to the back of the house where the bathroom was located.

Fonz stared at the board and saw that he really had no chance of winning that game. Bless had trapped his king from all angles. However, Fonz noticed that Bless's phone was still on the table. Just so happened, it buzzed as Fonz was looking at it. Fonz looked across the room and made sure that Bless was nowhere in sight and then quickly grabbed it. He looked at the text message that was across the screen. It was a message from a person named Watson. Fonz immediately knew it was the person that he was speaking to on the phone earlier.

The message read: 350k. I'll be by tonight to drop off. Talk soon.

Fonz heard the footsteps of Bless returning and quickly put the phone back in its original position on the table. Bless returned while drying his hands on his shirt.

"Another game?" Bless asked as he sat down at the table.

"I wish. I got a call from my mother while you were away. I have to check on her. She isn't feeling too well," Fonz lied as he abruptly stood.

"Oh yeah. Okay. Take care of your mother, for sure," Bless said as he stood up and reached out to shake Fonz's hand.

"No doubt. Thanks for the beer, homie," Fonz said with a fake smile.

"Maybe we can play again soon. I don't have too many friends, so a good game does good for my mental, ya know?" Bless said as he awkwardly shook Fonz's hand.

Fonz nodded his head in agreement, but cringed on the inside, knowing that Bless was *not* his type of company. Fonz couldn't imagine becoming friends with a square like him. Fonz would much rather rob Bless. And from what Fonz just saw, he knew that there was a very high probability of that happening in the near future.

The seed was planted, and the greed consumed Fonz's thoughts. He wanted to take what Bless had, and his mind had already been set. Fonz was about to put a play down on his boss. He saw a sucker in Bless, so he was about to hit the lick. Fonz had been waiting for a moment like this since he got out. He had been searching for a plan or a sense of where he was going. Fonz had finally got that. He had a plan now. It had been a long time coming.

Let's take a stroll down memory lane to see how Fonz got to this point . . .